The Fall of a Saint

Christine Merrill

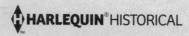

Recycling programs
for this product may
not exist in your area.

ISBN-13: 978-0-373-29776-4

THE FALL OF A SAINT

Copyright © 2014 by Christine Merrill

This edition published by arrangement with Harlequin Books S.A.

For questions and comments about the quality of this book, please contact us at CustomerService@Harlequin.com.

® and TM are trademarks of Harlequin Enterprises Limited or its corporate affiliates. Trademarks indicated with ® are registered in the United States Patent and Trademark Office, the Canadian Trade Marks Office and in other countries.

Printed in U.S.A.

www.Harlequin.com

"To be th___
duke wo___

He broke off.

There was the hesitation again, and proof that she was right not to trust him. She braced herself for whatever might come after.

"But would it not be better to be my heir?"

She could not help a single unladylike bark of laughter at the idea. Then she composed herself again and gave him a sarcastic smile, pretending to ponder. "Would it be better to be a duke than a bastard son? Next you will be asking me if it is better to be a duchess than a governess."

The room fell silent.

"That is precisely what I am asking."

* * *

The Fall of a Saint
Harlequin® Historical #1176—March 2014

Did you know that these novels are also available as ebooks? Visit www.Harlequin.com.

Dedication

To George Bloczynski,
who gave me my sense of humor.

Author Note

After you read this book, you will all ask the same question: What is Wow Wow sauce, and what does it taste like?

It was actually one of the hot recipes of 1817, published in *The Cook's Oracle,* by Dr. William Kitchiner. My heroine would be disappointed to learn that there is no evidence he was a real doctor. But he was famous for his dinner parties and his cooking.

Here is the recipe for Wow Wow Sauce:

"Chop some Parsley leaves very finely, quarter two or three pickled Cucumbers, or Walnuts, and divide them into small squares, and set them by ready; put into a saucepan a bit of Butter as big as an egg; when it is melted stir to it a tablespoonful of fine Flour, and about half a pint of the Broth in which the Beef was boiled; add a tablespoonful of Vinegar, the like quantity of Mushroom Catsup, or Port Wine, or both, and a teaspoonful of made Mustard; let it simmer together till it is as thick as you wish it, put in the Parsley and Pickles to get warm, and pour it over the Beef—or rather send it up in a Sauce tureen."

I recommend going light on the pickles and thinking of a really small egg when adding the butter, as those were the only things I could taste. I found it rather bland. But Kitchiner recommends a variety of additions, including shallots, capers and horseradish, for those who think it is "not sufficiently piquant."

Chapter One

'I am Mrs Samuel Hastings, but you may call me Evelyn.'

Maddie Cranston looked at the woman in front of her with suspicion. Mrs Hastings was smiling in a sympathetic, comforting way. But it had been her husband who had come to Maddie on that night in Dover with apologies and lame excuses, as though any amount of money could make up for what had happened. It was possible that Evelyn Hastings was just another toady to the Duke of St Aldric and therefore not to be trusted.

The duke had said she was a midwife. It would be a relief to speak to a woman on the subject, especially one familiar with the complaints of pregnancy. Sometimes Maddie felt so wretched that she feared what was happening to her body could not quite be normal. If anyone deserved punishment for that night, it was St Aldric. But if that was true, why did God leave her to do the suffering?

This stranger insisting on familiarity of address did not look at all the way one expected a midwife would. She was not particularly old and was far too lovely to have a job of any kind, looking instead like the sort of pampered lady who would hire nurses and governess to care for her offspring, rather than seeing to them herself. What could she know of the birthing and raising of children?

When one was surrounded by enemies, it was better to appear aloof rather than terrified. Life had proven that weakness was easily exploited. She would not show it now. She would not be lulled to security by a soothing voice and a pretty face. 'How do you do, Mrs Hastings. I am Miss Madeline Cranston.' Maddie offered a hand to the supposed midwife, but did not return her smile.

Mrs Hastings ignored her coldness, responding with even more warmth and, if possible, a softer and more comforting tone. 'I assume, since St Aldric sent for me, that you are with child?'

Maddie nodded, suddenly unable to trust her own voice when faced with the enormity of what she had done in coming here. She was having a bastard. There could be no comfort in that, only a finding of the best solution. She had been a fool to confront a duke, especially considering their last meeting. Suppose he had been angry enough to solve the problem with violence and not money? While she did not wish to believe that a peer would be so despicable, neither had she seen any reason to think otherwise of this one.

'And you are experiencing nausea?' the other woman asked, glancing at the water carafe on the table.

Maddie nodded again.

'I will ring for some tea with ginger. It will settle your stomach.' She summoned a servant, relayed the instructions and returned to her questioning. 'Tenderness of the breasts? No courses for the past month?'

Maddie nodded and whispered, 'Two months.' She had known from the first what must have happened but had not wanted to admit it, not even to herself.

'And you are unmarried.' Mrs Hastings stared into her face, as though it could be read like tea leaves. 'You did not attempt to put an end to this, when you realised what was happening?'

That was a possibility, even now. What future was there for her or the child if St Aldric turned her away? She would be a bastard with a bastard.

She stiffened her spine and ignored the doubts. If her own mother had taken the trouble to have her, she owed nothing less to her own child. The woman who bore her was conspicuously absent, now that wise counsel was needed. She did not wish to leave her baby without friend or family, to be raised by strangers as she had been. But what choice did she have? Her own presence in the child's life would make things more difficult, for it could not be easy to have a mother who was little better than a whore in the eyes of society.

An unmarried but powerful father was another

matter entirely. St Aldric had created this problem. Now he would be made to face the consequences of his actions. She returned her attentions to the midwife. 'No. I made no attempt to rid myself of the baby.'

'I see.' Mrs Hastings coloured slightly and changed the subject. 'And you are experiencing changes in mood, as though your mind and body are no longer your own?'

Now this was a question that could not be answered with a shake of the head, for it struck at the heart of her fears. She stared up at Mrs Hastings for a moment, then surrendered her courage and whispered the truth. 'I cannot seem to keep my temper from one minute to the next. First laughter, then tears. I have vivid dreams when I sleep. And waking I have the most outlandish ideas.' This trip was but an example. 'Sometimes I fear that I am going mad.'

The midwife smiled and relaxed into her chair as though pleased that they had found a topic she fully understood. 'That is all quite normal. It is nothing more than the upset of humours involved in the growing of a new life. You are not headed for the madhouse, my dear. You are simply having a baby.' As if there was anything simple about this, even from the first. The tea arrived, along with some flavourless biscuits. Maddie sipped and nibbled hesitantly, but was surprised to find she felt marginally better for the nourishment.

'It is a wonder that anyone does it at all,' Maddie

declared, taking another sip of tea. 'Much less allowing it to happen more than once.'

Mrs Hastings seemed to think this was amusing, for she made no effort to hide her laugh. 'You have nothing to fear from this point on. I will be here to take care of you.'

The woman could not possibly know what she was offering. But everything about her, from her softspoken words to the no-nonsense set of her body, was an assurance. Maddie risked relaxing into the cushions of the divan, if only for a moment. 'Thank you.'

'Before the onset of these symptoms, you had sexual congress with a man,' Mrs Hastings reminded her gently. 'Surely you understood what the ramifications of this behaviour might be?'

'It was not of my choice,' Maddie said, keeping her voice calm and level.

Mrs Hastings gave a small gasp of shock, but her smile remained as comforting as ever. 'Do you know the identity of the man who is responsible?'

This woman was different from her husband. Perhaps she could actually help with something more than ginger tea and kindness. Maddie decided to risk the truth. 'It was the Duke of St Aldric.' There. She had said it out loud. Even to admit it to one other person made the burden of the knowledge lighter. 'I was in an inn in Dover. In the night, he came into my room without invitation, and…' She was past crying about it. But to tell the story aloud to a complete stranger had not been part of her plan.

Evelyn Hastings's eyes opened wide again and her gentle smile turned incredulous. 'The Saint forced his way into your room and…'

'St Aldric,' Maddie corrected. 'He was inebriated. Afterwards, he claimed to have wandered into the wrong room.' But how was she to know if that had been true? Perhaps he said the same to every woman he casually dishonoured. In Maddie's experience, a title and a handsome face were not always an indication of good character.

Mrs Hastings seemed to think otherwise, for she was still staring in disbelief. 'You are sure about this?'

'Ask him yourself. He does not deny it. Or speak to Dr Hastings. He was there to witness it.'

Evelyn drew a breath, hissing it between her teeth. 'Oh, yes. I will most certainly ask my husband what he knows of this.' Her eyes were angry, but Maddie had no reason to think that anger was directed at her. It was more akin to righteous indignation for a fellow member of their sex. 'And you have no family to help you in this? No one to stand at your side?'

Maddie shook her head. 'I am alone.' There was no chance that the school that had raised her would take her back, after seeing what she had done with the training and education that should have got her a respectable position.

'Then you shall have me,' Evelyn said firmly, with a matronly nod of her head that hardly suited her. She rose from her chair as majestically as a queen. 'If you will excuse me, I must speak to my husband over this. And to the duke. It will all be settled once I am through with them.' Mrs Hastings drew herself up even taller, looking quite formidable, not just royal, but a warrior queen heading to battle. Then she disappeared into the hall, closing the door behind her with a resolute click.

Maddie smiled and settled back into the luxurious velvet cushions of the divan, sipping her tea. Perhaps Boadicea had arrived too late to fight for her honour. But she appeared more than able to gain reparation for the loss of it. Maddie need do nothing but wait.

Michael Poole, Duke of St Aldric, stood in the hallway of his London town house, one ear to his brother and the other tuned to the conversation taking place in the salon. He could not very well open the door again and demand that the ladies inside speak louder so that he might eavesdrop on them. But he had to know the truth, and the sooner the better. If there was to be a child, perhaps a son?

It changed everything.

'She found you?' His half-brother, Sam Hastings, was focused almost as intently on the closed door, staring hard enough to burn through it.

'She found me.' Michael had expected it, but not that it would come as such a relief. In each crowd he'd passed, he had wondered if he would see a pair of accusing eyes that should be familiar but were not. Now, at least, he had a name and a face to attach to that night, which had been but a blurry memory.

'I am sorry,' Sam said, as though he had anything to regret in this.

'You are sorry?' Michael laughed. 'What did you have to do with any of it?'

'It should not have happened this way. I should not have let her escape. The matter could have been properly settled in Dover. When I spoke to her that night, she claimed she wanted no contact with you, then, or in the future. I promised to respect her wishes. But I could have done more.'

'We had no right to keep her prisoner and force her to accept help,' Michael reminded him. The evening had been enough of a disaster. She'd have thought even worse of him if they had locked her door and demanded she stay until a proper settlement could be arranged.

'God knows, I tried without success to find her.' Sam was practically wringing his hands over the matter. 'England is a very large country and there are many unfortunate young women in it.'

An unfortunate young woman. Michael had never thought that his name would be connected to one who could be described thus.

'The fault is mine, not yours,' Michael replied. 'If I had drunk myself to unconsciousness that night, then I would not have caused her harm and you would not have had to bother to clean up my mess.'

'Or perhaps you could have remained sober,' Sam said as mildly as possible. 'No matter what you chose to do, we could not have foreseen the outcome.'

Had watching his father taught him nothing of the need for good behaviour at all times? 'I should have known better,' Michael insisted.

Sam gave no answer to this, which was probably proof that he agreed. Then he relented. 'You would never have sunk to this,' Sam reminded him, 'had you not experienced a shock from your illness.'

'I was upended by a sickness that would hardly bother a child.'

'The effects of the illness are not the same when the body has an immature reproductive system.'

'What a gentle way you put it, Dr Hastings.' Michael had lain for three days with a raging fever and balls swollen so that he could hardly bear to look at them, much less touch them. Then the disease had left him. But not as it had found him.

Or so he had thought.

Now, for the first time in six months, he had reason to hope. 'Miss Cranston has found me out and not because she is dissatisfied with your payment. She claims to be with child.' He paused to allow the doctor to conceal his surprise. 'Is that even possible?'

'Of course it is possible,' Sam said. 'I told you, from the beginning, that the negative consequences of the mumps on an adult male are not guaranteed. Yet you insisted on blundering through the countryside, inebriated and trying to prove your virility.'

'A bastard would have proven it well enough.' It had been what Michael had hoped for. The fear that a simple fever had destroyed the St Aldric line had turned to obsession. And from thus had come the hope that an accident with a member of the muslin set would assure him a fruitful marriage.

To announce such a thing to his own illegitimate brother showed how far he had fallen. Now that he was sober, the plan seemed foolish and cowardly. *Like father, like son.* It had been Michael's life goal to disprove the adage. He had failed.

'If you wanted a by-blow, it seems you will have one now,' Sam said, with a sad shake of his head. 'What do you mean to do about it?'

Michael was amazed that his half-brother did not see what was quite obvious. 'This current situation is much better than I'd hoped for.'

'You hoped to deflower a governess?' Sam realised how loudly he'd been speaking and dropped his voice to a whisper. 'And without her consent? Are you mad?'

'No. Certainly not.' Yet he had done just that. 'I never meant to enter that room. I lost my way.'

'Because you were too drunk to know better,' his brother reminded him.

He deserved the rebuke. His father had, at least, entertained himself with the willing wives of friends. But he had done worse than that. 'The woman I was seeking that night was hardly an innocent. Had there been consequences, she'd have been paid handsomely. I'd even have acknowledged the child.'

'As I assume you mean to do with this one.' Sam was offering the faintest warning that Michael must remember his obligations when dealing with the girl and her problem.

Sam had no reason to worry. After years of exemplary behaviour, Michael had made enough mistakes in the past few months to show him the ugliness of false pride and the lengths he must go to atone. There was no question in his mind as to what had to happen next.

The trick would be convincing the governess of it. 'If Miss Cranston is truly carrying my child, it need not be as an acknowledged bastard,' he said, cautiously watching for Sam's reaction. 'If I marry her and legitimise the heir...'

'Marry her?' Now Sam was staring at him with an ironic smile. 'Now I do not know whether to laugh or send you to Bedlam.'

'Why should I not wed her? Is there anything about the girl that appears she will be less than suitable? She is a governess and therefore educated. She is healthy.' And not unattractive. He was obligated to her. After what had happened, he owed her more than money. He should restore her honour.

'She probably hates you,' Sam said.

'She has good reason to.' He had seen the look in her eyes as she had confronted him with the truth. He would not have given a second thought to the woman standing in the street before his house. She was tidy to the point of primness, simply dressed in dark blue, and hair bound painfully tight, as though she feared it would do her an injury if a single curl escaped from the pins. The lips that should have been soft and kiss-able had been set in a determined frown and her brow had furrowed above her large brown eyes as she'd recognised him. Everything about her had announced her as just what she was: a disapproving schoolteacher.

She'd stepped in front of him, blocking his path as no one else in London would dare to do, and said quietly, 'I wish to speak to you about the consequences of your recent trip to Dover.'

The coldness in her voice still lingered with the memory of the words. But none of that mattered now. 'I will give her reason not to hate me. A hundred reasons. A thousand. I will give her everything I have. If the succession is to continue, I must have a wife and a child, Sam. There may be no better chance than this.'

The door beside them opened suddenly and Sam's wife, Evelyn, stepped between them, hands on hips. 'Explain yourselves, the pair of you. Tell me what that poor girl is claiming has no basis in fact.' She turned to her husband, growing even angrier. 'And that you had no part in this shameful business.'

Sam held up a hand as though to deflect his wife's wrath. 'I went with Michael to Dover, but only in hopes of talking some sense into him. As the Duke of St Aldric's personal physician, it is my job to keep him in good health, is it not?'

His wife responded with a frosty nod.

'He was showing signs of what I feared was chronic inebriation and had been—' Sam gave a delicate clearing of the throat '—doing things that I do not wish to discuss in mixed company.'

'Consorting with whores,' Evelyn said, refusing to be shocked. Then she stared at Michael. 'That does not excuse what happened to Miss Cranston.'

'It was all a mistake, I swear. I was on my way to visit someone else and took a wrong turning. It was dark….' That was hardly an excuse. He should have been able to tell the difference between the buxom barmaid he'd been seeking and the diminutive Miss Cranston, even without a light. But he could have sworn, as he had come into her bed, that she was willing and expecting him….

'When I realised that he was missing above stairs, I searched Michael out and heard cries of alarm,' Sam finished. 'By the time I found him, it was too late.'

Evelyn gave a noise of disgust.

'It grows worse,' Sam admitted. 'Miss Cranston, who, as I understand it, was a governess, was visiting the inn to meet with a future employer. The man arrived two steps behind me and witnessed the whole thing. She was sacked without references before she could even begin.'

Michael winced. He had but the vaguest memories of the last half of that evening. What he'd thought had been a thoroughly delightful interlude had ended in shocked cries, tears and shouting. And he had stood swaying on his feet in the midst of it wearing nothing but a shirt, with Sam looking at him much as he was now, in disappointment.

'I have been sober since that moment,' he reminded Evelyn. 'And I would have settled with Miss Cranston the following morning had she not fled the inn before we could speak to her again.'

'It is too late to concern yourself with what might have been,' Evelyn said with a shake of her head. 'It is what you mean to do now that matters.'

'Is what she says true?' Michael asked, not daring to hope. 'Is she with child?'

'To the best of my knowledge, yes,' Evelyn answered.

Michael took care to school his face to neutrality. It was wrong of him to be excited at the thought. Even worse, he was glad of it. To have a child.... Better yet, to have a son....

When he was gone, there would be a new St Aldric to care for the people and the land. And this boy would be raised differently from the way he had been. It was as if, despite his reprehensible behaviour, a curse had been lifted from his house.

'I said, what do you mean to do about it?' Apparently, in his distraction he had been ignoring his sister-in-law.

So he explained his plan.

Chapter Two

The muffled conversation in the hall droned on. Though she knew they were talking about her, Maddie felt oddly detached from the situation. In the time before Dover, she had avoided behaviours that might incite gossip. Her expectations were modest and her future predictable. She would teach the children of strangers until they grew too old to need her. Then she would find another family in want of a governess. At the end of it, she would have a small amount of savings to retire on, or stay on in a household so fond of dear, old Miss Cranston that they kept her beyond her usefulness.

But that seemed a lifetime ago. No decent family would have her after the scandal. It had been foolish of her to suggest that particular inn, but when her new employer had suggested meeting her stage in Dover, the temptation had been too great. She'd returned to the place several times as years had passed, knowing that, in her dreams at least, she would be young and free of the responsibilities of her oh, so ordinary life. She had gone to bed thinking of nothing but Richard and their last night together in the very same room.

The man who had come to her this time was no dream lover. It had begun sweetly enough, but it had ended in a waking nightmare. The drunken stranger had been hauled from her bed, while Mr Barker stood, framed in the doorway, shouting that no such woman should be in a decent inn, much less allowed near innocent children. The argument had moved into the hallway and she had slammed the door, thrown on her clothes and run as soon as she was sure of her safety. But not before hearing the name of her attacker, as he demanded, in a slurred voice, that this other common fellow stop raising a fuss over strapping a barmaid.

After two months of unemployment, she'd run through most of her tiny savings. Then there had come the growing realisation that she would share her future with another: one too small and helpless to understand the predicament they were in. So she had taken the last of the money and bought a ticket for London.

Now she was visiting the house of a peer. She glanced around her. While the decoration was as elegant as she might have expected, her presence here was beyond the limits of her imagination. Even in the parlours of the families that had employed her, she had not dared to relax. There were always children to watch and to remove to the nursery when their behaviour grew tedious.

The same strangers were once again settling her

fate in a public hallway, while she drank tea. Now that she had heard the truth, there was no sign that this Mrs Hastings would be easily silenced. There was a sharp sound of exclamation from her, as though one of the men had said something particularly shocking. Their muttered explanations sounded weak in comparison.

When a settlement was offered, Evelyn Hastings might serve as a mediator. She would know that decent people did not raise a child in secret and on a few pounds a year. A bastard of a duke deserved a decent education and a chance for advancement.

Maddie thought of her own childhood. The family that had taken her in had not let her forget that her origins were clouded. And the proper schools where she was boarded made no secret that she was there at the behest of an unnamed benefactor. There had been raised eyebrows, of course, but the money provided had been sufficient to silence speculation and the education had been respectable enough to set her on the path towards a career.

Surely St Aldric could do better than that for his byblow. There could be excellent schools, and a Season and a proper marriage for a daughter, or business connections and a respectable trade for a son. If the duke claimed his offspring, it would not be without family. One parent was better than none. Once she was sure the child's future was secure, she might quietly disappear, change her name and begin her life anew. No one need ever know of this unfortunate incident. She might be spared the snubs and gossip of decent women and the offers of supposed gentlemen convinced that, if she had fallen once, she might give herself again to any who asked.

It was for the best, she reminded herself, fighting down the pangs of guilt. The world would forgive St Aldric, and by association the child, but such charity would not extend to her. The door opened and Doctor and Mrs Hastings entered, followed by the duke, who shut it behind them.

Dear lord, but he was handsome. Maddie did her best to smother what should have been a perfectly natural response to the presence of him, for what woman, when confronted with a man like St Aldric, did not feel the pull of his charms? Apparently, God had decided it was not enough to give such wealth and power to a single human. He had made a masterpiece. St Aldric was tall but not thin, and muscular without seeming stocky. The hose and breeches that he wore all but caressed muscles hardened by riding and sport. Blue was too common a word to describe the eyes that stared past her. Turquoise, aquamarine, cerulean… She could search a paintbox for ever and still not find a colour to do them justice. The blonde hair above his noble brow caught the last of the afternoon sun and the hand that would brush the waves of it from his eyes was long fingered and graceful. But the clean-shaven jaw was not the least bit feminine. The cleft chin was resolute without appearing stubborn. And his mouth…

She remembered his mouth. And his arms bare of his coat, the fine linen of his shirt brushing her skin as they folded around her. And his body…

Her stomach gave another nervous jump. She remembered things that no decent woman should. And what she did remember should have not pleasure for her. That night had been her undoing.

Mrs Hastings saw her start and came quickly to her side, sharing the sofa and taking her hand. She was glaring at her husband, and at the duke as well, utterly fearless of retribution. 'Well, Sam, what do you have to say for yourself?'

A dark look passed between the couple, as though to prove an argument still in progress. But the doctor turned to her with the same sympathetic look he had given her in the inn as he'd led his friend away. 'Miss Cranston, we both owe you more apologies than can be offered in this lifetime. And once again, let me assure you that you are in no danger.'

But Maddie noticed the blocked door and lack of other exits. And the nearness of the fireplace poker, should Mrs Hastings prove unable to help her.

The duke saw her glance to it and made a careful, calming gesture with his hands. 'Miss Cranston,' he said, searching for words, 'you have nothing to fear.'

'Nothing more,' she reminded him.

'Nothing more,' he agreed. 'The night we met—' he began.

She stopped him. 'You mean, the night you entered my room uninvited, and—'

'I was very drunk,' he interrupted, as though afraid of what she might say in front of his friends. 'Too drunk to find my own room, much less that of another. I swear, I thought you were someone else.'

And her own arms had betrayed her, reaching out to him, even though an innocent governess could not have been expecting a lover.

'You called me Polly,' she said, almost as angry at herself as she was at him.

'I had an assignation. With the barmaid. And I was drunk,' he repeated. 'I had been drunk for several months at that point. What was one more day?' For a moment, he sounded almost as bitter as she felt, shaking his head in disgust at his own behaviour. 'And in that time, I did some terrible things. But I have never forced myself on a woman.'

'Other than me?' she reminded him. It was unfair of her. There had been no force.

But he must have seen it as such and counted her an innocent, for he looked truly pained by the memory. 'When I realised my mistake, it was too late. The damage had been done.' He took a deep breath. 'The night in question was an unfortunate aberration.'

'Very unfortunate,' she agreed, giving no quarter. But why should she? It was a lame excuse.

'Never before that,' he said. 'And never again. Since that day, I have moderated my behaviour. That night taught me the depths that one might fall to, the harm that one might do, when one is sunk in self-pity and concerned with nothing more than personal pleasure.' He was looking at her with the earnest expression she sometimes saw on boys in the nursery, swearing that they would not repeat misdeeds that occurred as regularly as a chiming clock.

She returned the same governess glare she might have used on them. 'That night taught *me* not to trust a door lock in a busy inn.' She needn't have bothered with the poker. The words and tone were enough to cow him.

'If there was a way, I would erase it so that you had never met me. But now I will make sure it stays in the past. Your reputation will be restored. You will never feel lack. Never suffer doubt. Everything you need shall be yours.'

Success! He was offering even more than she wanted. She would have a new life and another chance. 'For the child, as well?' she asked. For this could not all be about her alone.

'Of course.' He was smiling at her, as though there could be no possibility.

'We are in agreement, then? There will be a settlement?' She gave a grateful smile to Mrs Hastings, who had done miracles in just a brief conversation.

'The child will want for nothing. Neither will you. You need not concern yourself with a twenty-pound-a-year position in someone else's household. You shall be the one to hire a governess. You shall have a house, as well. Or houses, if you wish.' She did not need houses. He was becoming too agitated over a thing that could be settled simply. Perhaps there was madness in his family, as well as drunkenness.

Doctor Hastings saw her expression and responded in a more calming tone, 'You will be taken care of. As will the child. If the suggestions offered here tonight are not to your liking, you will have our help in refusing them.'

Evelyn Hastings nodded in agreement and squeezed her hands.

'Enough!' St Aldric cut through the apology with a firmness that seemed to stun both doctor and wife.

It did not shock Maddie. What could be more shocking than what had already occurred between them? The man was an admitted wastrel. It would not surprise her if he changed his mind suddenly and refused to pay, though it was quite obvious he had the funds. She raised her chin and stared at the duke, willing herself to be brave enough to see this through. Her mute accusation would be enough to break any resistance he might feel to help his own blood.

His blue eyes sparkled as he spoke, but not from madness; the light in them was as strong as blue steel. 'There will be no question of my acknowledging my offspring, Miss Cranston. There has been too much secrecy in my family thus far and it has caused no end of trouble. You have my word. The child you carry is mine and will have all the advantages I can offer him.'

'Thank you.' She had succeeded after all. Could it really be this easy?

'But…' he added.

Apparently not. What conditions would he manage to put on what should be simple?

'There is a complication,' he said.

Not as far as she was concerned. 'I will not speak of the beginning, to the child or anyone else,' she said, 'as long as you admit to its existence.'

'It is more than that,' the duke said, distracted again and pacing the rug before the fire. 'Six months ago. I took ill. The mumps. Had I been a child, it would have been nothing….'

'I am well aware of that, having helped several of my charges through it,' she snapped. 'But what would that have to do with our business?'

He continued, unaffected by her temper. 'As a result of the illness, I had reason to doubt that I would be able to produce issue.'

Now he was denying what had happened between them or questioning his part in the child he had given her. It was too much to bear. She used the last of her strength to draw herself up out of the velvet cushions to the unimpressive five foot four inches that she carried and stepped before him to stop his perambulation. Facing this man and being forced to look up into his face made her feel small, unimportant, weak. But she dare not appear that way, even for a moment. 'Do you doubt the truth of my accusations?'

He held up a hand. 'Not at all. I was surprised, of course. I spent the four months between recovery and our meeting in desperate and shameful attempts to prove to my own potency. It was on one such trip that

I found you while looking for a barmaid who was to meet me in a room just above yours.'

So he was a drunken reprobate, willing to lie with any woman to prove his manhood. It did not surprise her in the least. She folded her arms and waited.

'I do not claim to be proud of it,' he said, unperturbed by her disapproval. 'I merely wish you to know the truth. In six months, no other woman has come to me with the demands you are setting. I would have welcomed her, if she had. By the time I found you, I was quite beyond hope of that. I feared for the succession. Suppose I could not father a son? What would become of the title? The dukedom might return to the crown. What would become of my land and the people on it? They depend on me for their safety and livelihood. And if I could not do this one, simple thing...' He shrugged. 'I am the last legitimate member of my family, you see.'

She narrowed her eyes at the distinction. In her opinion, some people were too proud of their own conception, as if anyone had a choice in that matter.

'It is no excuse for what happened,' she said.

'I did not say it was. I merely wish to explain. That night, I'd expected to find a woman used to the risks of such casual encounters. But you are a governess, are you not?'

'I was,' she corrected. 'That is quite impossible now.'

'I understand that,' he said again. The sympathy in his voice sounded almost sincere. 'I do not mean to send you away with a few coins and a promise to take the child, as if you were some whore claiming to carry my bastard.' He took a step nearer to her and, unable to help herself, she backed away from him. Her legs hit the cushion behind her and she sat again.

Suddenly, he dropped to one knee at her feet. If it was an attempt to equalise their heights and put her at ease, it was not working. He was still too close. And though she had wished to bring the great man to his knees, it had been but a metaphor. The sight of a peer in the flesh and kneeling before her was ridiculous.

'You deserve better than that,' he said seriously. They were the words of a lover and her heart gave an irrational flutter. 'I meant to give you more and would have done had you but stayed in the inn until morning. I would have seen to it that no more harm came to you.' His voice was soft, stroking her jangling nerves. 'I never would have left you in a position where you might have to come to me and demand justice. But you ran before we could talk.'

She fought to free herself of the romantic haze he was creating. Did he expect her to take some of the blame for this situation? She would not. How could she explain the feelings of that night? She hardly understood them herself. Anger, fear, guilt and, dare she admit it, shame? Lying with another man was a betrayal of what she had shared with her darling Richard. That had been done in love. And she would never regret it.

But Richard was long gone, lost in the war. In his

honour, she had meant to keep the memory of that time pure. Now she could not manage to think of it without remembering St Aldric. 'I could not stand to be under the same roof with you a moment longer than was necessary.'

I ran. It had been foolish of her. But what reason had she to believe he would have treated her better than he had that night?

Of course, the man before her now did not seem as imposing as she had expected. He might actually want to help her. He was no less guilty, of course. But there was a worried line in his brow that had not been there when she had arrived. 'I understand why you did not want further dealings with me in Dover. I had given you reason to doubt me. But now I wish to make amends. You deserve more help than you received. So does the child you carry. I will not deny you, or him.' He was smiling at her. Had she not known better, she would have smiled back.

He continued. 'And to be the acknowledged bastard of a duke would open many doors. But...'

There was the hesitation again, proof that she was right not to trust him. She braced herself for whatever might come after.

'But would it not be better to be my heir?'

She could not help the single, unladylike bark of laughter at the idea. Then she composed herself again and gave him a sarcastic smile, pretending to ponder. 'Would it be better to be a duke than a bastard son?

Next you will be asking me if it is better to be a duchess than a governess.'

The room fell silent. Mrs Hastings stood and went to join her husband. The pair of them looked uncomfortable.

Now the duke was smiling in relief. 'That is precisely what I am asking.'

There was another long, awkward pause as she digested the words, repeating the conversation in her head and trying to find the point where it slipped from reality into fantasy.

'You cannot mean it,' she said at last. He was toying with her, waiting until the last of her courage failed, and then…the Lord knew what would happen. She would leave him this instant, running as she had before.

But her body understood what her mind could not and it refused to obey her. She tried to stand, but her legs could not seem to work properly. She made it partway to her feet, then sank back into the cushions of the couch.

St Aldric was unmoved from the place where he knelt before her. He waited until her weak struggle to escape had ended. Then he resumed. 'There would be many advantages, would there not? You would not need to fear disgrace or discomfort.' He was as handsome as Lucifer when he smiled, blue eyed and wonderful. His voice was low, almost seductive in its offer to remove all care. For a moment, she remembered how it had felt when he was on top of her, when it had still been a pleasant dream.

Before she'd known that what was happening was nothing more than lust.

'I would fear you,' she said bluntly and saw him flinch in response. The reaction, though very small, gave her a feeling of power and she smiled.

He continued, unsmiling and earnest. 'I swear I will give you no further reason to fear. Our son would have the best of everything: education, status and, in time, my seat in Parliament and all the holdings attached to it.'

'At this time, there is barely a child of any kind, much less a son,' she said. Duke or no, the man was clearly deluded. 'I am just as likely to produce a daughter.' In fact, she would pray for a girl, out of spite.

He shook his head. 'It was unlikely that you would have any child at all from me. I am sure this one must be a sign. It will be as it was for my father and his father before that, back very nearly to the first duke. In my family, the first child is always a male. If I have sired a child, it will be a son. And he will learn from me, as I learned, to cherish his holdings and be a better man than his father.'

That, at least, she could agree on. 'And to take care not to lose his way when frequenting inns,' she said.

The doctor and his wife both flinched at this, but St Aldric merely nodded. 'The next duke will be noble in title and character. He is far too precious to slight, even during the first months of his gestation. I want no question, no stain, no rumour about him, or his mother.'

He had added her, her disgrace and her reputation, almost as an afterthought to his mad plan. 'Am I to have no say in his future or my own?' She heard the Hastingses shifting nervously, clearly in sympathy with her, but she could not manage to look away from those very blue eyes.

The duke thought for a moment. 'You can refuse me, I suppose. But I will only ask again.' He reached out for her hand and she snatched it from his grasp. 'I need the child you carry.'

'Then take it and raise it after it is born,' she said firmly, sliding down the couch and looking away to break the hold he had on her. 'Give this child the advantages of your wealth and rank. But I will not be part of the bargain. I did not wish for this. I did not seek you out in that inn. It was you who came to me.' She could see by the shadowed look in his eyes that the truth of that still troubled him, and she took a dark, unholy pleasure in reminding him of it.

She looked up and saw the disapproving looks of both Doctor and Mrs Hastings, but their censure was not directed at her. If she refused the duke, his friends would side with her, just as they had promised. They had made the offer of help because they had tried and failed to dissuade him.

'No,' she said. 'The child is yours and I will not keep you from it. But you do not own me.' This time, it would be he who was alone to face an uncertain future.

'A son without a wife is no use to me,' he said, almost to himself. 'I do not need a natural child to be held apart from his birthright, as my father did to my brother.' He cast a glance in the direction of Dr Hastings, and Maddie noticed the resemblance between them that should have been obvious to her before.

The duke looked back to her. 'I need an heir. And I cannot marry another in good conscience after what I have done to you.' He reached out a hand to her again. 'Miss Cranston, you are not some common barmaid or London lightskirt. You were raised as a lady and are carrying my child. How could I offer less than marriage and still think myself a gentleman, much less St Aldric?'

He said it as if St Aldric were some superior being far above common manners and not simply the title he had been born with. She'd seen nothing saintly about him when they met. But suppose it had been a mistake? Perhaps he meant to do right by her after all. She felt a moment of relief, then counted it as weakness and batted the hand away. She must never forget who it was that offered and how long it had taken for him to find such remorse. This was not the time to be swayed by blue eyes and soft touches.

His hand dropped to his side, then rose again in supplication. 'I would ask nothing more from you than I have already taken. There would not be any intimacy between us. Once the child is born, you could leave if you wished. I would not stop you. I would not seek you out or force you to return to me.' He was still smiling. But there was a tightness in his face that made her think he would almost prefer it this way, so that he need never be reminded of how they had met. 'Let me give you the reparation I should have when we were still in Dover. I'd have married you then, had you but remained. Only when your honour is restored to you can this matter be settled.'

Since she had not stayed to talk with him, there was no telling if his words were true, or only a convenient afterthought that supported his current offer. But if he told the truth now, a single affirmative and she would be rich beyond care and she need do nothing more than she had already done. Her child would be safe and she would regain her reputation.

It was more than she had hoped for. And the offer was based on his assumptions that she had virtue to save other than the tissue of lies that her innocence had been, when he'd come to her. But she did not owe him details of something that had happened long before they'd met.

He noticed her hesitation and renewed his offer. 'I know I have no right to ask for it, but in exchange for your help, I would give you everything. Money. Jewels. Gowns. My name and title, and all the freedom that comes with it. If you wish it, it shall be yours.' His head dipped slightly, like a knight waiting to receive his lady's favour.

When she had set out for London, had she not

wanted to see him humbled? In one day, she had achieved her goal. But her victory had come too easy. The duke might appear to be a penitent, but he was still one of the most powerful men in England.

His modesty was an illusion, meant to put her at ease and win her cooperation. In a moment of carelessness, he had changed the course of her life. Now he thought that, in casually changing it again, he was doing her a service. But her true past would be lost to her: her job, her honour…and her Richard. This duke, handsome and kind as he might seem now, had ruined everything.

And no matter what she chose, his precious reputation remained untarnished. As he reminded her, even if he deserved punishment for his swinish behaviour, he was the legitimate son of a duke. The law could not touch him. Beside his power, the wishes of a governess who had been born on the wrong side of the blanket were as nothing.

But at least if she married him, he would not escape the past. She could be a continual reminder of his mistake. It was an appealing idea. And now he was offering her *everything*.

It was almost enough.

But suppose he found reason to change his mind? 'And what will happen if the child is not a boy?' she asked.

'It must be,' he muttered. 'Daughters in my family are few and far between. Why should it be different for me?'

Perhaps because he did not deserve such luck. He had done nothing to earn it. 'Enough of your problems and what you need,' she said. 'What if I bear you a daughter? Will you force your way into my room, as you did the last time?'

He flinched as if she had raised a whip to him and taken a strip of flesh from his back. Was it the reminder of their meeting? Or the possibility that she might carry a girl? Was the female sex completely valueless to him? His past actions certainly made it appear so.

He composed himself and raised his head to look at her. Then he continued. 'If you bear me a daughter, my promise would stand. All I ask is that you marry me. I can expect no more of you beyond that. In the event that the child is a girl—' he paused as though offering a prayer that it would not be '—I will explain all to the Regent and beg that he allows the title to pass through my daughter to her son. But I will not demand an act from you that you must certainly find abhorrent.' He was staring deep into her soul, willing her to give in.

If trust of strangers had come easy to her, she would have trusted this one. With eyes like that, so clear and blue, was it even possible to lie? And with the trust came the niggling desire to forgive him, to sympathise with him and to forget that she was the one who had been wronged. She could marry him and see that beautiful face each day for the rest of her life, those eyes gazing at her as though he cared.

Was she really so weak as that? He did not care. It was an illusion. 'You are banking on a male heir from a daughter who is not even born? That event, at a minimum, might be some twenty years hence. What guarantee do you have that you would be alive to see it? Or that the Regent will agree to any of this?'

'I will live,' he said. 'I will live because I must. I will have a son, or a grandson. I will not pass until I see the line established and know that there will be another St Aldric to take up the responsibilities of the holdings and the people who depend upon him.' With shoulders squared and jaw set in a way that displayed his noble profile, he stared past her as though looking into the future.

Was the title really so important to him? A man with such an extreme sense of his own importance might do anything to see success, even if it required him to destroy those around him.

It was a danger for her. But in him, it would be a weakness that might be exploited. 'You would not touch me,' she said cautiously, still searching for the trap in the words. 'And in exchange, you would give me…everything.'

'Anything you desire,' he said. He was holding his breath, waiting for her answer.

His friends looked alarmed. Perhaps they could see further than he did and realise the power he was giving her over his life. But Dr Hastings stepped forward and spoke. 'I can speak for my wife in this, I am certain. What he says is the truth, for though he might be guilty of other things, I have never known St Aldric to lie. If you feel, now or in the future, that he cannot hold to this bargain, we will take you in and I myself will call him out and defend your honour.'

The man was trying to make amends. And he was right in that it would be easier for the child, and for her as well, if they married.

But then she thought of Richard. She had loved, once in her life. It was a week that must last for ever, now that he was gone. She had long ago reconciled herself to the fact that there would be no children, no husband, no love for another until she found him again.

Was she willing to give herself, if not in body, then at least in law, to another man for the sake of convenience? It would render the past meaningless.

And here was the man who had put her plans for ever out of reach. She had not thought herself particularly spiteful. At least, not until she'd met St Aldric. Now he was giving her unlimited wealth and the power to set friend against friend. For a change, she held all the cards, to play or discard at leisure. Revenge was hers if she wished to take it.

But did she wish it?

The duke's hand still hovered before her and she reached out to clasp it. Had she expected the smell of brimstone when she touched him? A burn? A chill? This was nothing more than flesh and bone. He might be as handsome as Lucifer, but he was a mere mortal. And perhaps he was a fool.

His palm was warm and dry. As he rose and helped her to her feet, his strength made her feel safer than she'd felt since… She stopped the thought incomplete, for this man had nothing in common with Richard. She must never forget that, though the Duke of St Aldric might seem like a gallant rescuer, he was the cause of her current problems, not the solution. She forced a smile, imagining that she was strong enough to be his equal and not just a governess who had run out of options. 'Very well, then. I will marry you.'

And I will make you pay for what you have done.

Chapter Three

Was he sorry he'd asked? Not really, Michael reminded himself. If there was even the remotest chance
that he might gain a son from it, he was content to be
married. The identity of the bride hardly mattered.

Of course, it had not mattered before. Evelyn had
been suitable and he had liked her well enough. But
he did not think that what he'd felt for her could be
called love. He was not even sure he'd have recognised that feeling, had it come to him.

He was quite sure, however, that he did not feel
that particular emotion for Madeline Cranston. But
marriage to her was the right thing to do. He could
not choose another woman, knowing that this one ex-
isted and he had been the ruin of her.

He had made his bed with the unmaking of hers.

Of course, she had not asked for this situation
either. She had looked horrified when he'd first
suggested the plan. It proved she was not some empty-
headed fortune hunter. But she was a lady and in this

predicament because of him. He owed her. He must content himself with the fact that she was educated and not unattractive.

In fact, she was quite fetching when he could admire her unnoticed. She was more delicate than the women he normally favoured. The locks of chestnut hair that were not concealed by her bonnet formed lazy spirals, as though begging to entwine a man's finger. The brown eyes and gentle smile were just as lovely as he'd have hoped to see from a woman waiting for him at the altar.

It was only when she looked at him that the softness in her eyes became stony and the warmth of her smile turned glacial. It worried him that in the two weeks that he'd known her, the mother of his child had made no effort to be likeable.

A fortnight was no time at all. Soon she would see that he was not the beast she thought him. And then they might forge some truce for the sake of their child.

But suppose she did not mean to forgive him? To be tied to a woman who hated him for an indefinite future was as final as a trip to Tyburn. Worse yet, it was a repetition of his parents' marriage and the path he had vowed to avoid.

Even to the last steps, in the courtyard of St George's, Sam was questioning his plan. 'Are you sure, Michael, that there is no other way?'

'Are you suggesting again that I buy her off?' He stared steadily back at his brother, hoping that it would silence him.

'Of course not. The incident in Dover was badly handled by both of us. And now that you have found her again, you are not attempting to shirk responsibility. But she did not ask for marriage, Michael. Only that you care for the child. A settlement would have been sufficient.'

Damn Sam for offering such a reasonable solution. He could have given her what she sought, adequate funds to keep herself and raise his natural child. They'd never need see each other again.

Then he imagined his firstborn separated from him by a barrier of illegitimacy. His error might stand between the boy and his birthright. How naive he had been three months ago to think that a bastard would be nothing more than a demonstration of his virility with his half-brother as proof of how much trouble that might cause.

If there was to be a child, he could not imagine it anywhere but under his own roof. 'There is no other way that I wish to go,' he said, knowing it for the truth. 'I mean to marry the girl and protect the child.'

If his own childhood had taught him nothing, then Miss Madeline Cranston, soon to be her Grace the Duchess of St Aldric, would stand as a fresh reminder to him of what happened to those who strayed too far from the path of virtue. One might end up in a church, exchanging cursory vows with a stranger. But it was also a chance to start fresh. He would find a way to make peace with his wife. He would have the son he hoped for. The boy would be raised in an environment that was as far from his own childhood as humanly possible. That thought lightened his spirit as nothing else could.

Sam did not share his grand vision. His concerns were firmly grounded in the present. 'Was it really necessary to make such a public display of the wedding?' he asked. 'Pomp and circumstance will create more problems than they solve. Too many people have come to me already, asking about the woman and how you met her. How am I to answer them?'

'Ignore them. Soon there will be another scandal to attract the attention of the *ton* gossips and this will be quite forgotten.' Or so he hoped. When he'd offered for Miss Cranston, he'd imagined a quick ceremony in the family chapel would suit, and had pulled strings to get the special licence in record time. But that did not please his betrothed. Only the best church would do. And new wedding clothes, along with a full trousseau.

When he had reminded her that such things took time to arrange, she had responded, without a smile, that what was needed was money. She'd smoothed a hand over her still-flat belly and reminded him that time was of the essence. And since he had promised her whatever she wanted…

It had taken bribes, bonuses and additional fees all around. But the wedding and the pomp surrounding it had been ready within a week.

It was the first step towards a brighter future, he reminded himself, and fixed his face in the distant smile that would block even his only blood relation from prying further. 'If others ask about the circumstances of our meeting, our marriage or our future, you may tell them that it is none of their business. If they do not respect that, then tell them to come to me with their questions.'

'They wouldn't dare,' said Sam with a shake of his head.

'Exactly.' His brother was still too new to the family to understand how best to use the power of name and rank. 'The matter is closed.'

As long as they did not go to the duchess for the story. She might reveal the truth out of spite. She was waiting for him at the altar, watching him with a smile and a gracious nod.

Hypocrite, he wanted to shout. The loathing looks she gave him when they were alone were nothing like this one, which would seem to a bystander to be quite innocent.

In turn, he smiled back at her, playing the part of the eager bridegroom that society expected to see. He continued to smile as the bishop droned on about the sanctity of marriage and the need to procreate. The man had no idea what he was talking about. In Michael's experience, there was nothing particularly sacred about the unions he had seen. If his father had been a faithful man, he would not have left Sam as an unacknowledged, bastard son. Mother might have been quite different, as well. Michael had often imagined what it would be like to have an actual brother. But considering the chill silence that separated his parents when they were forced into company with each other, the lack of a sibling was not so very surprising.

Did his new bride have family? He had not thought to enquire. They were not here, at any rate. Nor were there friends. Perhaps she was as alone as he, the poor thing.

His mood softened. Then she turned slightly to look up at him. From a distance, the lavender gown she wore and the flowers in her hands reminded him of a *petit four*: small and sweet. But as he looked closer, the image faded. Though the colour suited her, the eyes staring up into his were dark, bottomless and intimidating.

She must have been a fine governess, he thought, for she was using her quelling stare upon him. He was far too old for that trick to work. The fierceness of her was an interesting counterpoint to her delicacy. He normally favoured fair women, but this one might have changed his mind. For all her dark looks, she had a sweet face and eyes that would melt him if she tried entreaty instead of demand. The child would not be unattractive, but possibly not tall. She was slight, fine boned and, thankfully, still slim. No one would suspect a pregnancy.

For a while. He felt another possessive thrill at the thought. It would not do to advertise her condition just yet. With Parliament out of session, they could retire to the country, finishing out the term of gestation in privacy. He had no desire to visit Aldric House, for the place held nothing but bad memories. Perhaps the future there could be different. The thought of the months ahead and the reward at the end of it had him feeling as giddy as a child waiting for Christmas.

'Your Grace.' The bishop's whisper hissed through the quiet of the church.

The vows. He had not been listening. Madeline glared all the more, as though he were the stupidest child in the nursery.

He smiled apologetically. 'If you would repeat the question, your Eminence?'

The bishop did as requested and Michael turned his attention to the business at hand, answering and repeating as charged with what he hoped was a confident voice.

Madeline Rosemary Cranston's voice was quieter, but no less steady.

Rosemary. Another omitted detail about his new wife. He would pay attention from now on. She might not enjoy his company, but he would give her no reason to fault it. When the bishop called for it, he offered the ring of braided gold that his mother had worn, watched as it was blessed, then took it back, slipped it onto her finger and promised to endow her with all his worldly goods.

There. The job was done, the knot was tied. They knelt and were prayed over.

Maddie seethed. He was the one who had wanted this wedding and he had not even been listening to the vows. To fumble over a simple 'I do' was a slight almost too great to bear. It was proof that he did not care about her at all. The marriage was just one more step that stood between him and his precious heir.

She calmed herself again, for it could not be good for the baby to always be so angry. The child had given her no reason for such bitterness. Its father had. But she would not blame an innocent.

The bishop was going on and on about fruitfulness and praying that God would endow her with a large family.

Her stomach twisted. One child with this man was more than she wanted. She had accepted that she was to live and die alone. The love she'd saved for the family she would not have with Richard would be doled out, a little at a time, to the charges she educated, for there would be no children of her own.

It seemed the baby she'd wanted would come after all, in a sham marriage to the stranger who had ruined her. *It is not too late to stop this.* The bishop had not finished the ceremony. Doctor Hastings had sworn to help her. He and Evelyn were there as witnesses. She had but to announce that she could not go on and they would take her in.

But what good would it do her to be alone to raise a bastard? The duke had made his feelings clear. He would persist until she surrendered and legitimised the child.

Now the bishop was speaking of submission, which was even worse than children. If St Aldric's goal was to have a woman in his bed, who had promised at an altar that she would not refuse, then she had played right into his hands.

A promise given under duress was no promise at all, she reminded herself. But all the same, her thoughts wandered back to that night, to awakening with a stranger.

She had been asleep and dreaming. It had been her favourite sort of dream. Richard had returned to her, just as he had said he would so long ago. Everything would be right at last. There was no job ahead of her, no more difficult children to teach. No more sour-faced parents expecting Miss Cranston to tend to the education of offspring that they could not be bothered to spend time with. After years without hope, she would be a bride.

And yet she had hesitated. 'I thought you dead,' she had whispered to him. 'In the Battle of New Orleans. There was no word of you after.'

'I am not dead,' he assured her. 'Just sleeping, as you are now. I am coming back to you. We will marry, just as I always promised. But tonight, it will be as it was before I left.'

She smiled and let her phantom lover ease her back onto the mattress. There was no pain, as there had been that first time. She was ready for him. She had been waiting for so long, for the long, slow glide of his body in hers. He was lying on top of her, his warmth taking the last of the chill from the winter air.

She wrapped her arms around him, feeling the

warm solidness of a man, whole and undamaged by battle. Two arms held her. Two legs tangled with hers. The lips on her throat were full and hot, the tongue tracing designs to the open neck of her nightshirt until it found her breast. If only for a little while, she was young again and happy. She sighed in relief as he entered her. She had been so lonely for so long....

She had given herself freely to him, returned his kisses and stroked his body, encouraging him to do as he would with her. She had climaxed with him, even as she realised that the voice crying out in triumph with hers was unfamiliar.

Then she had opened her eyes.

She was shaking again, with shame and self-disgust. She could pretend that the fault was all his, but that was not the whole truth. She had lain with a stranger. Worse yet, she had enjoyed it. She was everything she feared, a woman of no virtue and loose morals, no better than her mother had been.

Not now. She was in a church in London. Dover was as much a dream as Richard had been. She ordered her body to be still, but it would not obey, any more than it had on the night she had met the duke. She had been a fool to search out St Aldric and an even greater fool in marrying to spite him. If she was not careful, she would fall into his bed again, though there was no real feeling between them.

This could not go on. There must be some way to turn back the clock and return to the life she'd had. It had not been happy, but at least it had been predictable. She had but to open her mouth now, before the bishop pronounced the final words, and tell them it had all been a terrible mistake. But she could not bring herself to speak. She was trembling so hard she was surprised that the whole church did not see it.

Now she was swaying on her knees, very close to a full swoon. She gripped the communion rail before her, watching her knuckles go white with strain. Her vision narrowed as though she was at the end of a tunnel, looking down at the finger wearing the heavy gold ring.

The man at her side had noticed. He reached out and laid a hand over hers, as though he sought to comfort her.

She froze. If she put a stop to this, all of London would hear of the mad girl who had left St Aldric at the altar. She would be left with a bastard and a reputation not just tattered, but notorious. And he would grow in estimation to a tragic figure, undeserving of such horrible treatment. Beside her, St Aldric smiled and withdrew his hand. He thought he had quelled the shaking with his reassurance.

The man was insufferable. He had despoiled her memories of Richard and made her doubt her own heart. Then he'd left her in a delicate condition. He had trampled her life into dust. And now, though he cared less about her than he did the baby she carried, he thought all could be made right between them with a sham ceremony and a pat on the hand.

No matter what might lie in her future, she would

waste no more time in fear and trembling over the likes of St Aldric. And in marrying him, she would teach him the lesson he should have learned in the schoolroom: to do unto others as you would have others do to you.

Chapter Four

Michael stared into the glass before him, wishing that it held gin instead of champagne. It was far too early, in both the day and the marriage, to seek alcoholic remedy to the problems before him. If his current surroundings were a reflection of his future with Madeline, a strong drink at breakfast might not go amiss.

A church ceremony had cured the creeping sense of guilt he'd felt since the night in Dover. He had thought the worst was finally over and his life could return to normality.

But when Michael glanced out over the decoration of the feast she had arranged to celebrate their nuptials, he could find nothing normal in it. He must thank God for her good taste, he supposed. It could have been worse, had the surroundings been ugly. Of course, the level of excess was totally inappropriate for a wedding breakfast, which, in his opinion, should be small, tasteful and over quickly.

This had all the trappings of a masquerade ball. She had thrown wide the doors and cleared half the rooms in his town house to hold the crowd she had invited. Then she'd had the servants set every table in the place for guests. Every surface was decked with mountains of flowers, tropical orchids drooping on long stems from the midst of profusions of greenery. The walls were hung with ribbons and gold cages containing pairs of annoying, but beautiful, parrots.

Everywhere he turned little red faces looked down at him with beady black eyes. And whistled and chirped.

'Could we not have had doves?' he blurted, unable to contain his annoyance. Then, at least, the sounds would have been soothing.

'But, darling, doves are so common.' She gave him a pout worthy of a courtesan. 'And you said I could have anything. The guests are quite envious of it.'

The females, perhaps. All around him he heard awed whispers.

Lovebirds.... Very rare.... Straight from Abyssinia.... She bought every one on the boat....

The males looked as he felt, as though they were longing for a stiff drink to dull the effects of the squawking on their nerves. At least they did not have to pay for the damn things.

'It is a pity there was not time to teach them to speak,' she said.

He hid the flinch. With the evil smile she wore, he could imagine what she wished them to say. She wanted choruses of high-pitched voices accusing him of actions he could not defend. And doing it in front of what seemed to be half of London.

'A pity,' he agreed through clenched teeth. He could not shake the feeling, when he looked into his wife's triumphant eyes, that he was serving sentence for the crime. She must understand that this union was for the best. She was a duchess and not a gaoler. She had lost her position but gained a life of ease and a rank so august that no one would dare question her past.

Their lives would not be ordinary, especially not while they contained this many parrots. But they would be as far beyond reproach as any in England. That was all he had ever wanted for himself, and he had assumed by the way she lamented her lost reputation that it was what she wanted, as well.

He had meant to do little more than glance in her direction, to acknowledge her comment and prove that he was not bothered by it. But he had held the gaze too long, turning it into a battle of wills. For a moment, her confidence faltered and she looked as lost as he sometimes felt when under the scrutiny of this supposedly civilised society. Then she rallied and raised her guard again, looking as aloof as any lady of the *ton*.

Good for her. It had been rude of him to stare. Few men in London would have had the nerve to return such a look from a duke. But the little governess he had married weathered it well. None here would have guessed that, scant weeks earlier, she might have been a servant in their homes. She had best maintain that hauteur and let people think her proud. The more distant her treatment of society, the more desperate it would become to befriend her. If she was granted the gift of old age, she would be like those horribly intimidating dowagers that ran Almack's, casting fear into the hearts of all, lest some mistake on their part result in a fall from grace.

For now she was young and her antics, no matter how outrageous they might seem to him, would be copied as the latest fashion. It was beginning already. This morning, Hyde Park was empty, Bond Street was quiet and ladies who would be barely out of bed had dressed and forced unfortunate husbands, sons and brothers to dress and celebrate the marriage of St Aldric.

'It is good to see that you have found sufficient guests to share the day,' he remarked, trying not to think of the birds just above him that seemed to be following their conversation as though they understood each word. 'Are these people friends of yours?'

'No, darling,' she said with another false smile. 'I have no family. No acquaintances in town. No one to stand by me in my time of need.' She sighed theatrically.

It was another reminder of how low she had been when he had come to her. Despite the lack of money, family and position, Michael was beginning to suspect that he had never met a less helpless woman in his life.

She waved a hand to the assembly. 'These are your friends. I got the names from your housekeeper.'

He was tempted to sack Mrs Card for her help in this charade. She must have gathered every guest list in the house and combined them. Although he could recite their names from memory, he barely knew half the people attending. Which meant that along with the birds, he was paying to feed total strangers.

But the woman who sat beside him at a wedding breakfast fit for royalty was picking at her food as though it was so much garbage heaped on her plate.

'Do you not like it?' he asked, trying to mask his annoyance.

'You know I cannot eat,' she said, taking a small sip of wine.

And you know why.

She would not say it aloud, but she meant to dangle the truth in front of him like this, as though, at any moment, she might choose to announce to the whole of London how they had really met.

Was it just the circumstances of their meeting that had caused this vicious streak in her nature? Or had she been like this before, sour and disagreeable? His experiences with governesses in his own youth made him suspect the latter, for those he'd had had been a mirthless bunch. If so, she was not the sort of woman he'd have wanted to share his life and bear his child. If she hated the father, she would have no reason to love the son.

It was all the more reason to win her over, if it took

him a lifetime. He would do better than his parents had, in all ways. Madeline might have all the parrots she wished and gowns to match each feather. But he would abandon no son, as their father had done to Sam. Nor would he allow his home to degenerate into what his parents' had been, a battleground full of traps for the unwary.

If he failed? He glanced at his wife, chin stubbornly set as though she feared the food on her plate might leap forward on its own and attempt to nourish her against her will.

If she would not be swayed, then he had the resources to protect their child from her disdain. But the women put in charge of the nursery would be warm, affectionate and nurturing.

He spared a thought for Evelyn, sitting beside his brother at the other end of the table. Had things been different, she'd have been his, and a fine mother she would have made. She adored everything about children, even after seeing the birthing of them. He had been too particular last Season, while waiting for Eve to come to a decision. He should have offered for the first doting virgin he saw and got a ring on her finger. It would have saved him no end of trouble.

Of course, if he'd married Eve, he'd have made her terribly unhappy, for she had never loved anyone but Sam. She was beaming at her husband as though thinking of her own wedding, still sitting under her own honeymoon.

He wondered if receiving such devotion could raise

a similar response in his own heart. He had expected to be an amiable companion to any woman he married. But with so little previous experience, romantic love was quite likely beyond his ken. Without someone to show him the way, how would he find it? He looked speculatively at the woman beside him and tried to imagine her as his loving wife.

She looked back at him with annoyance.

It proved what he had often expected. If one wanted undying devotion, it would be wiser to get a dog than a wife. Madeline wished to be anywhere but near him and, at the moment, he wished to oblige her. 'It is a pity you are not well enough to travel,' he suggested, sipping his wine. 'A honeymoon journey at this time would be unwise. But now that the war is ended, a trip to the Continent would be lovely. Italy, Spain, France…'

For a moment, her glittering eyes softened. 'I have never been from England,' she said wistfully.

Did she have a weakness for travel? That was easily remedied and solved several problems at once. 'What a shame. I took the Grand Tour, of course. Or as much of it as was possible with Napoleon on the loose. I am sure it would be quite safe now, should you wish to visit the Continent.'

For a second, she looked positively eager. Then her eyes narrowed, her gaze piercing him like a gimlet. 'Oh, but, your Grace, I cannot possibly think of leaving you so soon. And there will be the baby to care for, as well.'

'He shall have wet nurses,' he reminded her. 'And governesses.'

'Oh, but I could not want to leave the training of *her* to strangers.' She emphasised the female pronoun ever so slightly, to remind him of the possibility that he might fail. 'I will be quite capable of educating our child. *Amo, amas,* amaretto…'

'Amat,' he corrected, unable to stop himself.

'I beg your pardon?' She gave him an innocent look.

'Amo, amas, amat. I love, you love, he loves. Amaretto is Italian. It is a bitter almond liquor.' Was she seriously as ignorant as she pretended?

'It does not matter, I am sure,' she said, her eyes wide and innocent. 'Love and bitterness are not so very far apart.'

It was a game, then. Another attempt to test his patience. 'While I have no doubt that you were proficient enough for your previous job, I thought you would not be interested in the education of our child,' he said, shooting her a triumphant smile over the rim of his wine glass. 'You mentioned you wished to leave me soon after the birth, did you not?'

Apparently, there was something in what he'd said that upset her. For a moment, all pretence disappeared and her composure cracked. She looked confused and frightened. Worse yet, she looked ready to cry.

He held his breath and prayed the mood would pass. People around him were supposed to be happy and at ease. He made sure of it. He knew even less about womanly tears than he did of love. Perhaps Madeline sensed it and was resorting to tactics far more upsetting than tropical birds and bungled Latin.

Then the moment passed and she made a little pitying click with her tongue. 'You agreed that I could do just as I pleased. If it pleases me to leave you, I shall. But not because you are bribing me with trips abroad. Suppose I wish to stay?' She gave a feminine shrug. 'Perhaps you could send me away against my will. I know what you are capable of. I am sure your friends would be interested in hearing it.'

At last he was on familiar ground. He smiled back at her. 'Why, my dear, one might think that you married me for no other reason than to await a chance to tell that story.' Let her deny it, or admit.

'It will be a nice change for you. When we met, you seemed most eager to ruin your own reputation. I simply mean to be the helpmate you deserve.'

It was a pity that her plan would not work. Men of his rank would be better, were it possible to shame them into good behaviour. He took a sip of wine. 'Then let me avail you of the sad truth, Madeline. You are as ignorant of the *ton* as you pretend to be of Latin. The reason for our marriage does not matter to them. Not really. They will gossip for a time. But they would not dare cast me off for my piggish behaviour. Men and matrons will applaud me for marrying you and not leaving you to your unfortunate fate. And women of a certain, liberal-minded sort will find me dangerously appealing. Do your worst. Tell your story, here, now, before the cake is cut and your audience departs. And then we will get on with our lives.'

He took another sip of wine, enjoying her shocked silence and waited for the farce to end.

When the door closed on the last of the guests, Maddie could not help the feeling of relief. It was foolish and spiteful of her to attempt to goad a reaction from St Aldric in full view of the *ton*. Other than the few tart remarks he'd made to her, he'd taken it all with amazing sangfroid, as though it were perfectly natural to have his house and his life turned upside down by a stranger.

She had almost got to him when she had bungled the Latin. He had been marched through conjugations and declinations by a governess at least as strict as she was and had been unable to keep from correcting her. But it went too far against her grain to perpetuate such deliberate ignorance.

Perhaps that was what had upset her so. The knowledge that the only child she was likely to have would be raised by others. It was the best thing for the baby, of course. St Aldric could provide more than legitimacy to the little one. But to know that there would finally be someone who she could honestly claim as family and love as her own, only to walk away....

It was too soon to think about any of this. Much could happen between now and the birth. Her head was not clear enough to imagine the future. The servants had begun to clear away the mess. As the orchids disappeared towards the kitchen, she could take her first free breath. The cloying perfume had very nearly sickened her at the table and she had managed only a few bites of ham and the thinnest slice of wedding cake. And her head still rang from the sound of the birds.

That had not worked either. He had ignored the chirping and whistling. But judging by the murmurs of the guests, the *ton* would declare this the event of the Season. By tomorrow, matrons all over London would be stalking the docks in search of imported birds.

She was the only one who had suffered by this day. As she always did on visits to the town house, she felt small, insignificant and very much alone.

It had been easier in the past week, staying with Evelyn and Dr Hastings. Their house was elegant, but nothing so large as this. She felt almost at home there, after she got used to the novelty of sleeping in a room decorated for a guest and not a servant. Evelyn was both wise and helpful, putting her mind at rest on the subject of pregnancy and delivery. Doctor Hastings was quite different from what she had expected him to be, after Dover. He'd made it clear that his home was at her disposal for as long as she might wish it.

She had dared to imagine, just for a moment, that they were her family. To be so welcome and not obligated to work for her place was a novelty. Nor did she think St Aldric had paid them for their hospitality to her, as her absent father did the family that raised her. They took her in willingly, expecting nothing in return.

Then Dr Hastings had hinted, very diplomatically, that if she had a change of heart about the marriage or anything else, she was to come to him and he would help her.

It made her uneasy. Did he think her not good enough for the duke? Was he hoping, in the guise of kindness, to dissuade her from marrying his brother? Or did he know facts that had not yet been revealed to her and meant this as a rescue? It could be that St Aldric was just as dangerous as she expected him to be and that marriage to him would be a fresh misery.

But it was too late to worry now. She had chosen to marry him. Despite what a villain her husband might be, she was a duchess and she meant to behave as capriciously as the worst of them.

When she had demanded that a modiste must drop everything and provide a wardrobe fit for the wife of a peer, St Aldric had hardly blinked. Instead, he'd added, 'You will need a maid, as well. Do you wish Mrs Card to arrange suitable candidates for you to interview?'

A devilish part of her had decided that enlisting the housekeeper was the way to cause the most difficulty. But it left her in the embarrassing position of interviewing servants, using a tone that had been used upon her scant months ago. In the end, she chose one of the housemaids who had some experience with dressing and hoped for the best.

That girl, as the others had, accepted her as her future mistress with eager enthusiasm. She seemed to think any woman that might suit his Grace was near to perfection.

How could they all be so wrong about him? Was he truly able to hide the darker side of his nature to all but her? The servants seemed to view him not so much as a saint but almost as a God, rushing to do his bidding as though it was an honour to serve here.

Such misguided loyalty chilled her blood. And with it went any desire to upset the household instead of the master. These poor unfortunate souls had done nothing to deserve her punishment. She knew from experience what it was like to have employers with no sympathy for the servants and the difficulty their outlandish requests might make. She could make their lives hell with unreasonable demands. Or she could set the whole house into chaos by her inaction.

But there was something in the steady, cold gaze St Aldric had given her when he had introduced her to the staff that made her doubt the effectiveness of such a trick. The house would run on without her, she was sure, just as it had before there was a duchess.

If she had a grievance with their master, it would not be solved by taking it out on others. So today, she politely thanked Mrs Card for the extra work necessary to arrange a feast on short notice, then announced that she would retire to her rooms.

She gave a brief, helpless look to the woman. 'Someone must show me the way.' If she had come to marry in a normal way, would she still be ignorant of the bedrooms on her wedding night? Certainly not if it had been Richard, as she had hoped. She doubted that the man she had wed would be so particular about preserving his lady's honour once she had agreed to a marriage.

It made her think of Dover and the deliciously familiar sensation of a man inside of her, followed by the shock of discovering a stranger.

The housekeeper noticed her nervousness and smiled, sympathetic and cheerful. 'Of course, your Grace.' But where Mrs Card saw the excitement of a new bride, Maddie struggled with feelings of embarrassment and guilt still mixed with the low, erotic hum inside her, the desire to give herself over to sin, just to be as alive as she had when she had been with Richard. She did not want to be alone.

But neither did she want to be trapped in a mockery of a marriage. And the smiling housekeeper only made her feel guilty. Did this poor woman not realise her true feelings for the duke?

Apparently not, for the trip to the bedrooms was peppered with congratulations and good wishes, and the hope that there would soon be a child at Aldricshire, for his Grace had been so hopeful of that....

'Of course,' Maddie answered with a smile that felt even more false than usual, and continued up the stairs. They would realise, soon enough, the reason for the marriage. Rather than being shocked at her lack of chastity, they would probably applaud the coming of another little duke.

The housekeeper stopped at an open doorway with an expectant smile. 'Here, your Grace, are your rooms. They have not been used since the duke's mother was alive. But we have aired them and Peg is already unpacking your things.'

As though it would make her feel the least bit at home to think of St Aldric's mother, who probably had blood as blue as her son's eyes. 'Thank you, Mrs Card. I am sure I shall be fine now.'

With a bob the woman retreated, leaving Maddie alone. Or as alone as she was ever likely to be, for there was still a servant in the room. Her new maid was industriously filling drawers and searching for things that might need mending or pressing. As if that was even needed. The clothes were all new.

Too new. Though they belonged to her, Maddie felt no comfort in having them. She'd found the most expensive dressmaker on Bond Street and had nearly bought out the shop. The woman was frustrated by her lack of interest in the details and her instance with quantity over style. In the end, she'd had the same design made in multiple colours, so eager was she to get away from the swatches and the measurements and the assurances that this or that fashion would bring out the colour in her cheeks or accent her particularly fine figure.

The clothes were like the food at the feast today, beautiful, expensive and unpalatable. The room was overflowing with more clothing than she could ever have time to wear. St Aldric did not seem bothered, but the sight of the gowns made her feel guilty and wasteful.

She missed her old clothes. The dull and inoffensive wardrobe appropriate for a governess had been comfortable. Her maid, Peg, had set them aside with a sniff, and Maddie had not seen them since. She suspected, if she searched the shops frequented by the servants in this area, she would find that Peg had sold them.

Before they had gone, she'd managed to save a grey shawl, arguing that it was both soft and warm, despite the bland colour. She'd also salvaged a wrapper that she'd stitched herself out of dark blue flannel. Peg argued that it was not the least bit romantic. She much preferred the lacy pelisse that was meant to go with a nearly indecent gown. God forbid his Grace see the horrid blue thing; he would return to his rooms and not come back.

That was precisely what Maddie hoped. She reached for the shawl, rubbing it against her cheek for comfort as she examined her new room. It did not matter if it had been unused for years. It was a testament to quiet elegance, the green-striped silk on the walls and the cream satin of the coverlet, the gleaming brass of the candlesticks and the well-oiled wood of tables and cabinets. In comparison, her clothes were as garish as the parrots in the ballroom.

Peg did not seem bothered by them in the least. She

plucked the shawl from her mistress's hands and ran an admiring hand over the gowns in the cupboard. 'You have so many nice things, your Grace. So much nicer than the old ones. And the gown you are wearing now does not need a shawl.'

'The neck is too low,' Maddie muttered. Peg had declared it decent for church. But it still felt too low, too light and far too frivolous.

'It was no lower than the other ladies were wearing,' Peg said firmly. 'And much prettier. Though it is a pity that it will not fit for long.' She eyed Maddie's midsection speculatively.

'I don't know what you mean,' Maddie said bluntly.

The girl blushed. 'It's all right, your Grace. There is very little that a lady's maid does not notice and even less that she talks about.' She touched the gowns again. 'The dressmaker did not allow much in the seams, but I will have to let out the bodices soon enough.'

'I am only just married,' Maddie insisted.

'It's all right,' Peg repeated. 'You can hardly be blamed for getting an early start with a man like the duke.'

'Why is that?' There was little point in denying further what Peg would see with her own eyes each time she was dressed.

'He is a most handsome man,' the maid said with a giggle.

'Is he prone to…?' How best to ask this question? It was better to be prepared than to find out more unfortunate truths and be surprised by them. 'I do not know him well at all, really. People think so highly of him that it is hard to believe the truth of it. What sort of master has he been to the household?'

'The best one in London,' Peg said with a grin. 'In all of England, most likely. Kind, thoughtful and never has a sharp word for anyone.'

'There are so many in the peerage that abuse their power,' Maddie said as delicately as possible. 'They are given to all sorts of excesses. Drink, gambling, women...' She waited, hoping that the desire to gossip would prove too great to resist.

The girl gave her a wide-eyed look, as though she could not imagine such a person. 'Then we are doubly fortunate to be in this house.'

'Working for a man with no vices?' She had seen for herself that it was not true.

The girl paused for a moment, as though wondering how much she might admit to. 'There were some dark times, after the illness. Brooks, his Grace's valet, was quite worried. But his Grace is right as rain now.'

'And these dark times—were there events that I should know of? Problems with the household, perhaps?' The man had all but admitted his need to prove his virility. He must have started under his own roof.

To this, Peg's only response was an incredulous laugh. 'Oh, no, your Grace. Certainly not. He was far from home is all. And missing from Parliament, which was not like him. He is most diligent about that. And we are always glad to have him here, for it is a point of pride that we work for him. The duke is a perfect gentleman.' She leaned forward, as though she was afraid to be caught gossiping. 'He does not like it much, but the people here in town call him The Saint because he is so generous and good.'

'I would prefer not to hear that particular nickname in the house.' And there was the supposed saint, standing in the doorway that must connect their bedrooms.

The maid started at her master's voice and went hurriedly back to straightening the folds of the gowns she was hanging.

'I would not worry, for you will not hear it from me,' Maddie said, staring directly into his eyes in challenge.

'I did not think I would,' he said in a dry tone and glanced to the maid.

She curtsied, ready to leave the happy couple alone, and Maddie resisted the urge to grab for her arm and demand that she remain. She was not ready to be alone with the duke.

St Aldric stood his ground, leaning against the door frame, neither advancing, nor retreating. 'That's all right, Peg. You may stay.'

There was no logical reason for her to fear him, but her heart was in her throat to be in a bedroom with him again. It created a weird mixture of terror and excitement to remember his touch. He knew her as only one other man had. But unlike Richard, who she had loved with all her soul, St Aldric was still a stranger to her. He did not seem equally bothered. But he had known many women. What did he even remember of her, other than that she carried his child? And how much of that night did she remember clearly herself?

She did not want to remember it. It was over. They were together because of an accident, she reminded herself. A mistake. And the duke's weak character. And she would not allow it to happen again, for another night in his bed would mean that she was little better than a lustful animal.

She focused her mind on a battlefield far away, and a good man lying in an unmarked grave. Then she stared at the duke, safe and whole and undeserving. 'You wished something, your Grace?'

He smiled. It seemed normal and natural, and she heard the maid sigh at the sight, for the duke was even more handsome when he chose to smile. But Maddie could see it for what it was: a polite mask hiding whatever it was that he actually thought when he looked at her. 'I only came to suggest that you dress to go out. It is a fine afternoon and I thought we take advantage of the weather to purchase your wedding present.'

Chapter Five

A gift.

Maddie hardly knew what to say to that. Courtesy had the words *you needn't have bothered* rushing to her lips. She had taken so much already. The gowns…

A duchess cannot wear rags, she reminded herself. The breakfast…

A social success.

And the ring on her finger, heavier and more magnificent than anything she'd ever hoped to have.

And entailed, the voice in her head said firmly. If he wished to buy her something that was truly hers, then why should he not? It was a bribe to keep her silent and in good humour.

When he had retreated into his own room, Peg chose a smart walking dress of pale blue muslin and a bonnet trimmed in silk cornflowers. Admiring herself in the mirror, Maddie could not help but smile. While she did not feel like a duchess, in this simple gown she felt less like a governess in fancy dress.

Then she went downstairs to find St Aldric waiting in the hall wearing buff breeches, Hessians and a wine-coloured coat, along with the same unflappable smile he had been using in her bedroom. He was so polite she might as well have been a stranger.

As he glanced up at her, it faltered, but not with the annoyance she'd expected to see when she caught him unawares. He was staring at her with admiration.

In response, she could feel herself colouring. The most handsome man in London was looking at her as though he was eager for her company. Lord help her, she was smiling back. Her steps quickened on the stairs, hurrying to his side.

Then she remembered her resolution in the bedroom less than an hour ago. She must not forget who she was, who he was and what had brought them to this. He remembered as well, for the look in his eyes faded, the sincere smile faltered like a guttering candle and the false courtesy returned.

She nodded in acknowledgement, wiping the smile from her own face, and allowed him to hand her up into the seat of his high-perch phaeton.

If there was any trace of excitement in her, he could attribute it to the carriage. The vehicle was as impressive as everything else about St Aldric: expensive and elegant, it was so new that the paint was barely dry. But the unsteadiness of it wore on her nerves. Suppose they were overset? Was such a conveyance safe for anyone, much less a woman in her delicate condition?

She considered fussing about it, or offering some

snide comment implying that he meant to kill her on the very first day of their marriage.

But he handled the ribbons himself and it might be unwise to upset him while he drove and create the accident she worried about. They were travelling at as spritely a pace as could be managed through the busy streets of London, but he navigated with confidence and took no foolish risks. As she watched him, so obviously skilled, she felt that creeping admiration of him that rose in her whenever she did not stop to remind herself what a complete bounder she had married.

'Where are you taking me?' She tried to sound petulant, but the words came out as curious and excited.

'Tattersall's. You cannot be a smart woman of the *ton* without a curricle of some sort, or at the very least a mare to ride in Rotten Row.' His smile was serene and distant, but she noticed the faintest smirk at the corner as he added, 'I expect it will be very expensive.'

That might have been the case. Perhaps this was a peace offering to her, formed in a way that saved face for the both of them. If she meant to spend his money, here was a chance.

Then he added, 'At breakfast, Rayland mentioned some fine stock he has up for auction today and I do not want to miss a chance at them.'

So that was it. He had been talking horseflesh on his wedding day when they were barely out of the church. He was making a public show of her wedding gift, so that anyone keeping a tally of correct marital behaviour would not be shocked that he had abandoned her at home to go to an auction.

Her feelings meant nothing to him. If he'd have asked her, she'd have announced quite truthfully that the thought of handling a carriage herself, or even parading on the back of some blood mare, was terrifying. She knew little of horses and even less of driving. To develop such skills while with child went against all common sense. If he'd wished to torture her, he could not have found a better way.

It grew even worse when they'd arrived at their destination. St Aldric handed the reins to his tiger and helped her down into a throng of men, hounds and horses. It was loud, dusty and intimidating. With the huge beasts stamping the dirt on all sides of her, she was near to panic.

And that was the only reason that she found herself clinging to his arm, as though his presence would be any kind of security at all. It was degrading. She hated having to ask him for help. Before they had met, she had made her way in the world alone, using good sense to avoid situations that were not safe for an unattached female. After Richard had left, she'd been scrupulous of her own safety and her honour. But if being the Duchess of St Aldric meant that she would be dragged into such places and forced to rely on her husband for security, then she was likely to dislike this marriage even more than she'd expected.

Even worse, her husband was patting her hand, as though her frailty was to be assumed. 'You needn't worry. The horse I have in mind for you will be far more easy than these brutes. We will find you a mare as gentle as a lamb.'

Of course he would. He would not wish to risk the safety of his child after all. The thought brought the bitter taste back to her mouth that she had not had since Evelyn began dosing her with ginger.

She took a deep breath and mastered it. 'Am I to have no say in the purchase?'

He looked down at her, surprised. 'I did not think you knew horseflesh. If you wish, you may decide what you are able to handle.'

It was a dare, she was sure. A society lady would show spirit and choose some impossible horse and he would laugh at her attempts to control it. He led her towards the auction, examining the mares that would come up for bid. They were big but gentle, with soft dark eyes and velvety muzzles, nuzzling gently at her to see if she'd brought them treats. They were not lambs, precisely. Rather like extremely large dogs.

She still did not like them. Nor did she like being so far from her element. But he was as content bartering for horses as he was when she'd turned his home into an aviary. It seemed he was at ease in any situation.

She would always be a step behind. A little lost. Struggling to catch up, even in situations she had orchestrated. At the wedding breakfast, he had greeted each person in the throng she had invited by name, deflected any congratulations that had seemed less than sincere with praise of his wife's taste and intelligence and even spoken knowledgeably when questioned about the lovebirds. He managed to be all things to all people.

Except to her, of course. She had seen the true man in Dover. What she was seeing now was nothing more than false coin. If everyone else was fooled, then London must be populated by idiots.

At the moment, the patron saint of the *ton* was too busy checking teeth and feeling withers to notice her annoyance. He led her down the row, pointing out a shoulder here, a fetlock there, pulling back lips and staring into eyes, giving no hint as to what was good or bad, treating her as though she might have some idea of what she was supposed to be looking at. He was making fun at her expense, waiting to see her prove her ignorance.

She let him carry on with it, refusing to take the bait and speak. Then she glanced past him, outside the gates.

In sad mimicry to the auction here, which was made up of the finest horseflesh in London, a group of farmers and drovers had gathered to make their own trades. Although there were probably some solid plough horses in the bunch, even she could see that many of the animals were as poor as their owners. One or two of the men moving through that crowd were bidding often and buying so many beasts that she suspected their purchases would be nothing more than hooves, hide and glue by the end of the week.

St Aldric took no notice of that sale. He was too preoccupied by the thrill of the chase on his side of the fence, gauging his competition and readying his bids for horses worthy to carry his new wife.

She sniffed. Horse mad, just like the rest of his set. He was likely to fritter away more money than she could imagine for the right to own more animals than he could possibly need. More proof that she had been a fool to try to shock him with her gowns.

She wandered away, in the direction of the drovers' auction. Her husband did not notice at all, but the groom, seeing her depart, hurried after. It was nice to know that someone truly cared for her safety.

Seeing the horses here was almost comforting. They were no smaller, of course. In some cases, they were truly massive. They needed the height and weight to pull ploughs and wagons. But at least they were calm.

It was the calmness of animals resigned to their fate that drew her. They stood between the traces, plodding forward at the pull of the reins. At the end of the journey, they did not come to a green pasture like the fancy horseflesh that her new husband admired. These animals, with their rheumy eyes and drooping heads, were headed towards the knackers. She thought of her own life in service and how it might have ended, too old to be useful and full of employers rather than friends. She turned in sympathy to pat the nearest horse.

It was the most flea-bitten, spavined nag she had ever seen. Its owner hung back from the crowd, obviously dreading the likely response when it was brought up for bids. When the poor thing was led to the front, there were snickers and catcalls of 'too thin for dog meat' and 'not fit for glue'.

She felt sorry for the owner, who looked even more dejected at the prospect of being unable to sell it. Bidding began, with the auctioneer's suggested forty pounds greeted with resounding silence. He followed it with thirty, then twenty, then ten. His voice grew more desperate with each suggestion. Still, the prospective buyers said nothing. The farmer who held the harness looked near to tears, at least, what she could see of him. As usual, she was small and short, and losing sight of the action with each shift of a head in front of her.

Finally, she could stand it no longer. 'Fifty!'

There was a gasp from the men around her and heads turned to find the source of the bid. This resulted in much muttering and rustling in the crowd, and bodies pressing in on her, making it even harder for her to see. She pushed forward, darting under armpits and working her way to the front.

'I am not sure I heard?' the auctioneer called. 'Did someone bid?'

'Sixty!' she cried again, louder so that her voice might carry over the laughter of the mob.

Someone shouted something about a madwoman in the back and she pushed hard against the man ahead of her, moving forward another few inches. 'Seventy!' She was at the front now, staring at the auctioneer as the nag puffed steamy breath into her hair.

'Excuse me, miss,' the auctioneer said with a toothy grin. 'It seems you have wandered into the wrong place. The proper auction is through the gate, yonder. And just past is the Jockey Club, if you are looking for a rider.'

Judging by the laughter around her, the comment was as rude as it sounded. She ignored it. 'I want a horse. This horse. And I am willing to pay eighty pounds for him.'

'Her.' She spun to attack the yokel behind her who dared to point out her ignorance and found herself staring directly into the chest of her new husband. 'The animal in question is a mare.'

She doubted the men around her knew who was in their midst, but she could tell from the hushed silence that they recognised rank and quality.

'Begging your pardon, my lord,' the auctioneer murmured, 'but the lady… I do not think she understands the principal of an auction, or the worth of the animal.'

'One hundred!' she said to the auctioneer. She turned back to St Aldric, staring up at him and daring him to correct her. 'You said I could make the decision.'

'So I did,' he said, with the slightest of sighs. He turned to the owner. 'How much do you wish for this...horse?' He seemed almost unwilling to acknowledge the sex of the animal before him.

'It is an auction, not a sale. And I bid one hundred,' she reminded him.

'The beast you have chosen is not worth half of that.'

The farmer was too shocked to speak for himself, but Maddie held her ground, unwilling to be forced into a reasonable price. 'Fifty? That is far too little for a beauty like this.' She stroked the animal's nose and it responded with a sort of confused gratitude, as though unsure of just why a human would touch it so gently. But it submitted, fearful of arousing ire.

She smiled at St Aldric again, who looked as though he was embarrassed to be seen standing next to such a pathetic animal. That was enough to decide her. She gave him an empty-headed, society smile and gushed, 'I simply must have her.' She turned the horse's head so that the mare could display a mouthful of worn, yellow teeth. Perhaps this was what he had been trying to show her in the others, for surely this horse stood as the bad example by which she could measure the others.

'This is a cart horse,' the duke said patiently. 'I wished to buy you a decent mount. Or perhaps some carriage horses. I have no idea what you mean to do with this.'

'I shall name her Buttercup,' Maddie said, with evil glee. If only for the colour of those horrible teeth.

The duke gave the same resigned sigh he'd made

after each of her outlandish requests and reached for his purse. 'One hundred pounds it is, then. If my wife wishes.' He glanced around at the crowd, who were leaning in as though expecting him to buy again. 'But this is the only purchase she will be making today.' Then he spoke to the farmer. 'If my groom gives you direction, can you bring the horse to my stables?' He glanced at Maddie and said, in an undertone, 'Or would you prefer that I carry her there on my back?'

It was another sign that he knew exactly want she was doing, but it was delivered in such a benign tone that it was clear no damage had been done to him. 'No, the delivery shall be enough, I am sure. Settle her in our stables, so that I might visit her at my leisure.' She stared at St Aldric, blinking innocently. 'Will she not look magnificent in Rotten Row, next to all the other fine horses of the nobility?'

'I am certain she will draw just the sort of attention you wish,' he replied.

'I shall want a carriage, as well,' she said, baiting him again.

'I am sure we can find a vehicle that will suit. A milk wagon, perhaps.' He turned and walked away and she had to hurry to keep up. For a moment she feared that he might abandon her here, surrounded by strangers and dangerous animals. And then he glanced back at her, offering his arm and proving that, once again, his perfect manners made him impossible to goad.

Chapter Six

Supper was a chilly affair in the main dining room. Michael debated taking it in his room, after making some lame excuse about the busy day and the need for rest. Even if that was true, it would appear that he was running from his wife. And she would think she had won.

Peers were supposed to be made of sterner stuff than that. If he could manage the interminable arguing of Parliament, he could learn to ignore the behaviour of the stranger he had married. With sufficient time and patience, perhaps she would learn to tolerate him, as well.

For now, she was picking at her food, even when there was nobody but him to see it. It made him suspect that, just perhaps, her apathy towards the delicacies of the breakfast was not feigned. When she chose, it was the things that were bland and easy to digest. The roast that had been prepared was going to waste. Her plate held poached fish and potatoes and she'd kept the soup bowl, which held thin broth. With the small breakfast, and the fact that he'd dragged her away from luncheon and tea to stare at horses, she'd eaten close to nothing.

No matter their differences, he could not stand by and watch her starve. But how to get her to eat? He turned to the footman waiting beside his chair. 'This is all delicious, of course. You can assure cook that I have no complaints. But I am feeling rather unsettled. Perhaps a baked egg or two would do the trick.' He glanced up as though it was an afterthought. 'Would you like one as well, my dear?'

She looked at him with relief. 'Thank you.'

The sincerity seemed to surprise them both. As the servant went to get the dish, they fell into silence again.

When the eggs arrived, she tasted one cautiously and set her fork aside.

He thought on it, for a moment. If heavy foods did not suit, and plain foods did not interest, what was left? He reached for the tureen of Wow-Wow sauce and ladled it liberally over his eggs, then offered some to her.

She sniffed suspiciously. 'What is this?'

'The latest thing. Cook says it is a recipe from a Dr Kitchiner. He seems to take a very scientific approach to cookery.'

'A doctor, you say?' She looked hopefully at the ladle.

'It is probably quite healthy,' he assured her. By the taste of it, it was a testament to the idea that what did not kill strengthened. But it was devilishly addictive and unlikely to make her feel any worse. He held his breath as she served herself and took the first bite of egg.

She smiled. She chewed. She swallowed. Then she reached for more. He watched with relief as she smothered her food in the stuff and ate with enthusiasm. Then she followed the main course with brown-bread ice cream and a shockingly powerful Stilton.

He felt a little of the tension within him relax. After breakfast, he'd wondered if she meant to starve herself just to spite him. It appeared that, once awakened, her digestion was like her will, made of cast iron.

He was enjoying his port when she pushed the last empty plate away, stifling a yawn.

He stood. 'It is late and you are, no doubt, tired. May I escort you to your room?'

Her eyes narrowed, suspicious, but she rose and nodded, preceding him from the room. She hesitated at the turn in the hall, and again at the head of the stairs, proving that his help had been necessary. She barely knew her way around the house without help. He made no effort to call attention to it, but did not leave her until they'd arrived at the door to her room, which he opened and held for her.

When she was through, he followed and shut it behind them.

She gasped and he held up a calming hand. 'I only

wish a moment alone to speak with you before you ring for the maid. Then I will be gone.'

'Very well, then,' she said, frowning. 'Speak.'

He ran the risk of undoing the good that had been done over dinner. But life would be easier if they aired their differences sooner, rather than later. 'I would like to know your intentions towards this marriage and to have an honest explanation for your behaviour.'

Surely she could not pretend ignorance. He gave her a pointed look. 'For example, are the antics of this morning likely to be repeated?'

'Antics?' she said, with her most wide-eyed, innocent stare.

'The elaborate and unnecessary gatherings?'

'You did not think it important to celebrate our marriage?'

'I am surprised that you did,' he said. 'We both know that you did not wish to marry me. This afternoon, the unfortunate horse…'

'You promised me freedom to do as I wished,' she reminded him.

'I did,' he agreed.

'I mean to do so.'

'I see.' He took a breath. 'And you may do as you like. But I do not understand it. Are these things truly what you want? Or are you attempting to bother me with them?'

She stared at him, unwilling or unable to answer the question.

'It matters not one way of the other,' he assured her.

'I doubt there is a punishment you could devise that I have not already wished upon myself. The man you met that night in the inn... It was not me.' It sounded ridiculous when he phrased it that way. But it was the truth as he saw it and he meant to repeat it until she believed him.

'You deny that you attacked me?'

'It was not an attack,' he said. Then he took a moment to calm himself, for he did not wish to appear angry with her for something that had been his fault alone. 'It was a mistake. It was me in body. I do not deny that. At the time...' He was pausing again. 'My behaviour was so out of character that I view the man who was so misguided as to enter your room as a virtual stranger to all I stand for, all I believe and all I hope to emulate.'

'But it was you all the same,' she responded, clearly unimpressed. 'Who you were, before or since, does not matter to me. It is who you were on that night that affected me.'

Of course that was true. It was naive to hope that they could put this behind them so quickly. Had his father not told him that it was a man's actions that stood after his words were forgotten? Old St Aldric had no right to lecture about character. Father had been guilty of a number of ignoble actions far worse than the night in Dover.

And that was the problem. There was much good his father had done in life. The other, older lords spoke of his speeches with respect and sometimes even awe.

But Michael could remember none of that when compared with the man he had seen in Aldricshire.

The same would not be said of him. He bowed his head to his wife, as a show of contrition. 'I am sorry beyond words. I would take it back in a heartbeat, if there was some way.'

'To keep me from distrusting you?' She stood, frozen on the doorstep, staring at the connecting door between the rooms.

'You will never need fear me,' he reminded her.

But she did. Her voice held none of the bravado he'd heard earlier. She had finally eaten, but she was still pale and so tired that she swayed on her feet.

'You have my word,' he promised again.

'I prefer more concrete examples. Is there a lock on my bedroom door?'

He gave a sigh of exasperation, wishing he'd had it pulled out years ago, as he'd done with the lock on his own door. 'There is one fitted there already.'

'To which you hold the keys,' she reminded him.

'We will change them, then,' he said. 'First thing in the morning. The door to the hall and the connecting door between our rooms, as well. I will have no key made for myself. Even the housekeeper shall be denied one, if that is what you wish.' It would be embarrassing. All in the household would know that he was denied access to a room where a husband ought to hold dominion.

The memory of being on the wrong side of a locked door was all too familiar.

'That is tomorrow. What of tonight?' she prodded, totally oblivious to his feelings. If one had nothing to hide, or nothing to contain, then one had no need to lock doors. And until this moment, his London home had been blissfully free of them.

The fact that he had no desire to enter her room did not matter. It was the appearance of the thing that was important to her. He reached into his pocket and removed the ring of keys that opened and closed her half of the master suite. 'Here. This is yours to hold, if it makes you feel more secure.'

She took the keys and he saw the furrow in her brow smooth. 'Thank you. And now, if you will excuse me?' She glanced towards the door.

'Of course.' He gave a small bow and exited through the hall door, turning to the left and entering his own room, only a few feet away.

Once he was safely alone in his room he took a second set of keys from his pocket and set it on the bureau. He stared at the ring for a moment before deciding that the keeping of it was not quite a lie. She had demanded the door keys and he had relinquished the duchess's set.

He smiled grimly. If she had thought to demand all keys, he would have relinquished the duplicate set meant for the duke. But she had not. He was in his right to stay silent.

And in his right to refuse her request. He had promised her complete freedom and what very nearly amounted to a pledge of obedience to her wishes. No matter the fact that she had earned it, it went against the natural order of things to be so womanly and submissive. He would be damned before he was locked out of even a single room in his house, for her or anyone else.

What she had really wanted was a promise from him not to enter. She could have taken his word on that. The demand for the key was a slap in the face of honour and never something he'd have expected from a wife. Did she want him to nail the door shut, to prove his intentions to avoid it?

Instead, it gave him the perverse desire to block it open, if only to prove that he was strong enough to stay on his side of the threshold.

But he did not wish to turn an uneasy truce into an argument. Nor did he have a reason to knock on the door and request further communication.

He had no reason to talk to his wife. That he should say such a thing on his wedding night was almost beyond his understanding. He turned back into his room to prepare for bed.

When he opened his eyes again, the room was still dark. Far too early to rise, especially after the trouble he'd had getting to sleep. He was annoyingly aware of the stranger sleeping in the next room. There was a presence where there had always been an absence. The occasional sounds of movement as Madeline prepared for bed. The muffled conversation with the maid and the close of the hall door as that servant departed. And then there had been nothing. Even the faint glow of candlelight at the crack under the door had dimmed.

It was not loud. But it was more activity than he was used to in this most silent part of the house, and he was not sure that he liked it. That was strange, for he had always hated the silence that came with total privacy. It was a reminder of the fact that he was alone.

Now he was not alone, and it had not been the magic cure to bring peace and an end to the insomnia that sometimes plagued him. Instead of feeling free to relax, he felt responsible for the source of the noise, worrying that she could not sleep either and wondering if there was something he might do to help. It was only when he was sure she was asleep and silence had come again that he had finally been able to close his eyes.

Something had awakened him. A sound of some sort, he suspected. Did she snore? It would be a nuisance, but he would adjust. Then he heard the sound again. It was not a snore, but he could not place it. Perhaps it was someone in the hall. Or maybe Madeline had summoned her maid. It was definitely a female voice, coming from the other side of the locked door. But he had not heard the hall door open. Nor was there an answering voice.

This was the sound of Madeline in conversation with herself.

She was an odd woman, was she not? Did she do

this often? Did she not realise that he could hear? The droning repetitiveness made him think that she was talking in a dream. She could hardly be blamed for that. He did not sleep easily in a strange place either.

Gradually, the one-sided discussion was becoming an argument, louder, faster and more agitated. Was he obligated to intervene in some way? If he rang for a servant, he would get his valet, who would then summon her maid. Half the house would be awake before she was. And in that time, the dream would continue to distress her, for she showed no signs of waking or easing back into sleep.

He threw aside the covers and padded barefoot to the dresser, rummaging around in a drawer for the key to the adjoining room. He had promised not to bother her. But perhaps, in this instance, it was better to do so than to leave her in distress. Once she was quiet, he would put the key away and they could both sleep in peace.

Through the door and into her bedroom, he found his way to her bedside without effort. He knew this room, as he did all the others, better than she ever would. But why she slept with the bed curtains pulled tightly shut, he could not decide. It must be stifling within, for the night was showing the first heaviness of summer air.

He pulled one back with the rattle of curtain rings and whispered, 'Madeline, are you well?'

'No,' she moaned. 'No. Stop.'

'Madeline.' He said her name louder, for she had

not heard him. 'You are dreaming. There is nothing to fear.'

'No,' she said again, although it was impossible to tell if she was speaking to him. 'Richard. Where are you? Come back to me.'

Who was that? She had not mentioned a brother, a cousin or anyone else by that name. 'Richard is not here,' he said patiently. 'It is only me.'

'No.' She tossed on the pillow, her head turning towards him, then away and then back again. 'Richard.'

She was getting louder. If he did not do something soon, the servants would come and find him standing over her bedside, watching her suffer. And she was suffering. Her lip trembled and her skin was pale, but beaded with perspiration. No matter the differences between them, it pained him to see her thus. In her sleep, she was distraught and even an enemy did not deserve that.

'Madeline.' He reached out and touched her shoulder.

She started. Her eyes were wide open now, still sleeping, and she was scrambling away, up the bed to wedge herself against the headboard, clinging to the curtain as though it was a shield. 'Not Polly,' she insisted. 'Not Polly. Who is she?'

It was him. In her nightmares, she was back in Dover. And she'd awakened to find him looming over her, just as she had that night.

He backed away. 'I'm sorry. So very sorry. I heard you cry out. I meant no harm.'

'Not Polly,' she gasped one more time, her eyes still sightless, trapped in a dream. 'It is me, Richard. Don't you remember?'

'You are having a nightmare,' he said, feeling more helpless than any other time in his life. 'You are safe here.' Safe from him. How odd that he should need to say it.

'Richard?' she said hopefully. Her eyes were closing again and there was the slightest hopeful smile on her face. 'You are not dead after all.'

'Yes, love. It is Richard. I am here.'

'Then take me away from here. So unhappy.'

He could give her everything but the one thing she truly wanted. He must remember that he was not the only one in this marriage who had known disappointment. Michael wet his lips and lied again. 'Of course, love. We will go back to where we were happiest.' Wherever that was. The words seemed to help. She settled back into the pillows with a sigh, her features relaxing.

He stared down at her for a moment, unable to look away. Had he never seen her happy before? He had known she was attractive, but he had not seen the beauty of her smile. So soft, so sweet and welcoming. And not for him at all. It was for a man who had not been there to protect her, when she'd needed it most.

Then he noticed the tears drying on her face. He had caused those. He ran the tip of a finger over her skin, smoothing them away.

She leaned her cheek into his hand, her lips grazing his fingertips in a kiss.

He froze, afraid to move. If she woke and caught him in her bedchamber, there would be no hope of gaining her trust. But dear God, it was sweet. Though he had more power, rank and money than any sane man might need, he envied this Richard, who once had the devotion of his little Madeline.

Very carefully, he pulled the covers back up and tucked them around her, gently wiping away a curl that was stuck to her damp face. 'Sleep well, darling. Everything is all right now.'

And it would be all right. He would see to it.

Maddie blinked awake to find the morning sunlight shining bright through the crack in the bed curtains. She had been dreaming again, she was sure. Her arms and legs felt heavy and tired as though, in her sleep, she had walked a great way.

At least she was not tangled in the sheets today. Some mornings she awoke paralysed in body as well as mind, so sad that she could hardly fight herself free of her own blankets.

Last night's dream, as she'd remembered it, had been different from what it had been in the past. She was at the inn in Dover, of course, but she had not lain with a stranger. There had been no shame. No embarrassment. Once again she had felt young, innocent and in love. It had been so real that she was sure she had been awake. To find a man standing over the bed should have frightened her, but strangely it did not. For though she could not see his face, she had been sure it was Richard. He spoke softly to her, calming her, and she'd wondered whether he'd finally returned, just as he had in the dream.

Then she noticed the change in him. She had kissed his hand, but he had not joined her on the bed. Instead, he'd stood over her for a moment, then arranged the blankets and eased her back to sleep as though she were a frightened child.

It was not the Richard she had known. It had been an angel. She could not see the wings, but she was sure they must have been present. Before he had gone, he'd promised to protect her and she'd believed him. He would always be here for her, guarding over her.

If dreams had meaning, this one said she must stop waiting. She was married now. Her true love was not coming home as anything but a sweet memory. It should have upset her, to have the last hope dashed. But he had told her, in the dream, that she had nothing to fear. She must trust him, just as she had when they were together. And with that knowledge, she had made peace with his absence and drifted deeper into sleep, waking refreshed.

It was odd that she should have the first restful night in so long while in the very house of the man whom she least wanted to see. But as he had promised, he had not bothered her in the night. There was the security of the locked door between them. Before she had climbed into bed, she had turned the key and set it aside. A few minutes later she had checked the door. And then she'd checked it again. Then, finally, she had crawled into bed, pulled the curtains and rolled away from it, vowing that she would not touch it again until morning.

It was foolish to doubt herself about such small things. Perhaps it was the life growing inside her, urging her to check and double-check each thing she did, as though testing her abilities to keep the young one safe. It was nonsense. The door was locked and the key was still on the dresser.

But who was to know if she assured herself that it was indeed locked, just as she'd left it? She climbed out of the bed and walked to it, took the knob in a firm grip and twisted slowly and silently, so as not to awake the duke. But instead of resisting, it turned easily, opening suddenly towards her because of the weight resting on the other side.

The Duke of St Aldric tumbled into the room.

She took a step back, clutching her wrapper in alarm and trying to disguise the ridiculously lacy nightgown that Peg had insisted she wear on her wedding night.

He was even more surprised than she. He looked up at her with sleep-dazed eyes, not quite sure of what he was doing on the floor.

'What is the meaning of this?' she demanded.

But the meaning was obvious, if still confusing. On his side of the door, a bench had been set to block the threshold and the duke had been using it as a bed.

He had been sleeping sitting up, leaning against the door. When she'd opened it, he'd fallen backwards.

'Bloody hell.' He was rubbing the back of his head now, glanced up at her and glanced hurriedly away as though not sure where he could politely look. He struggled to disentangle himself from the bench so that he could regain his footing.

She should have done the same. For while her modesty was mostly preserved, his was not. The expanse of his chest was bared where the dressing gown fell open. As the skirt of it flapped in his movement, lengths of naked leg were exposed, clear to the groin. Long, well-shaped legs, with firm calves and thighs.

Dear lord. A trail of gold hair, curling down the centre of his body, well past his navel, disappearing beneath the belt and leading to the tiny bit of his body still obscured by his robe—and the fabric that did nothing to hide the bulge of morning beneath it.

Then the moment had passed and the man was on his feet in the doorway, adjusting his clothing and properly covered.

They stood for a moment in silence. His eyes were unwavering, locked to hers, cool and gentlemanly.

It took all her strength not to look down again, to see if any trace of that glorious male body was still visible. Lust, pure and simple, was added to the many curious feelings that seemed to rise and fall in her like the tide now she was with child. Despite what had passed between them, she had to admit that her

new husband was a beautiful specimen and worthy
of admiration.

And one who looked as though, if he had less than
perfect poise, he would have been shuffling and stam-
mering at the awkwardness of this encounter. 'I heard
you cry out in the night. You were clearly quite dis-
tressed.' He gave the belt of his robe another tug.
'When I had assured myself that there was no real
danger, I returned to my room and remained there,
against the door, in case the dream recurred.'

'You. Entered my room?' The angel that she had
felt watching over her in the night was him? And then
he'd returned to his side of the threshold to guard her
as she'd slept.

'I meant no harm.'

It had not been Richard at all. It had been St Aldric again. She had grown used to finding him in her
nightmares. But must he invade the happy dreams,
as well? She could feel her cheeks growing red, not
just from embarrassment, but anger. 'The door was
locked.'

'There is a second key.'

'In your possession.' What point had there been in
giving her her own key, other than to create a false
sense of security in her?

'I will not be denied entrance to rooms in my own
home,' he said, his demeanour cooling by the minute.
'You must trust, on my honour, that I will not use it
but in the most dire emergencies.'

'And you discovered such an emergency on our very first night of marriage?'

'You were crying out loud enough to wake the household,' he said almost in a whisper. 'It was emergency enough for me.'

'It was only a dream.'

His eyes refused to meet hers, for they both knew what the cause of her nightmares had been. 'I will give you the key,' he said, reaching into his pocket.

'And how can I trust that there is not a third resting on your keychain?'

'You have my word.'

'Which you have already broken by hiding this from me. I demand that you move me to a different room immediately.' Preferably one on a different continent. Then perhaps she could escape the warring feelings of anger, confusion and guilt. At least if she were far away, she could free herself of the desire to look at his body again. She forced herself to focus on his face, just as he did for her.

As she watched, a variety of emotions moved across the perfect features like clouds over a clear sky. He was embarrassed, ashamed of what he had done at Dover and the lie he'd just told her. He considered something for a moment, rejected it, considered something else and seemed to settle on something. When his eyes lifted to hers again, they were dark, but far from unreadable. He was angry. As though he was being forced into something disreputable that he wanted no part of.

'It would be difficult to move you in this house, as the guest rooms, while lovely, would hardly suit the size of your wardrobe. But if we remove to Aldricshire, you will have the solitude you request. The lord's and lady's chambers there do not connect.'

How odd.

She'd very nearly said it. Or made some other foolish comment about the inconvenience that must cause. For while it was customary to have the nursery as far away from the adult rooms as it was possible to be, she had never heard of a husband and wife sleeping so obviously apart.

Until her own marriage, of course.

'That would be most suitable,' she said. It should be, for there was clearly something about the idea that upset him. That had been her object in marrying, had it not? To see to it that he was as miserable as she had been.

But why should sleeping apart from her make him unhappy? She'd made it clear from the first that there would be no communion between them. He was a fool if he expected he could change her mind by keeping her in London.

'I would like to leave as soon as possible,' she added, not wanting to tempt fate by the continued sight of him in the morning.

His mind calculated. 'After breakfast, then. The trip can be made in less than a day. We will travel lightly. Our luggage will be sent after.'

As though expecting her to offer some devilish

objection to this, he corrected, 'My trunks, of course, can follow. You are likely about to tell me that you cannot be expected to travel without a wardrobe. I will have Scott bring up the cases and instruct your maid to begin packing immediately.' He turned to the bell pull, ready to rearrange his life to suit her whims.

It seemed he was not inconvenienced in the least. He acted as if there was nothing in his schedule that could not be postponed or handled by another. It would be her fault if this trip broke her goodwill with the servants. After the work they'd put into the breakfast, the sudden move would create even more chaos.

If the servants had been surprised by this sudden upheaval, they had the grace not to show it. Footmen who had been pulling down the flowers in the ballroom were recommissioned to carry boxes from her room to one of two waiting carriages. They even smiled while lugging heavy trunks up and down the stairs. Apparently, if the duke requested something of one, it was treated as an honour to comply.

When she had enquired as to the need for two vehicles, she was informed that the second held her clothing. The first was for her and her maid.

And the duke?

Preferred, at least on this instance, to ride. As they set out, she saw him holding the bridle of a brute of an animal with eyes that flashed like the very devil. It was black and glossy, so different from the nag she had chosen on the previous day that one might even wonder if they shared a species.

St Aldric mounted without the help of a groom, swinging easily up into the saddle and then glancing to her where she sat in the carriage, so high that he had to look down to her, despite the height of the rig. Then he turned the horse and set off at an easy pace down the drive.

Though Peg seemed to think it an eternity, the trip was not to be particularly long. 'Nearly forty miles,' she breathed. 'I have never been so far from home in my life.'

Maddie hid her smile. Changes in position had forced her to criss-cross the country on several occasions. Before that, she'd not had a true home to miss. 'It is much easier this way than to travel in a mail coach,' she said. 'It is never nice to have one's schedule set by others and to be chased in and out of highway inns with barely time for refreshment.'

'If you need either, the duke says you must be sure to ask and we will stop immediately,' Peg replied.

Maddie frowned. He had said so, had he? Not to her. Although it seemed that he'd had no problem relaying that concern for her comfort to the maid.

When she mentioned that it might be nice to stop for lunch, the caravan drew immediately to a halt and one of the outriders produced a cloth for the ground and a basket of dainties that was more like a feast than a picnic. She dined on potted pheasant and champagne, a nice Stilton and strawberries that she was assured came from the vines that grew right in Aldricshire and were shipped each week to London. There was even a small pot of the medicinal sauce that the duke had offered her, and it seemed to make each food more appetising. She even tried a bit on one of the strawberries when she was sure no one was looking, and was surprised to find them sweeter than usual.

The only thing absent from luncheon was the duke himself. He had lagged far enough behind that she was assured he must have stopped at one of the inns they had passed.

Maddie frowned. Perhaps his fine black horse was not so fine after all. It could not even manage to keep up with the carriages. Or perhaps he was not satisfied with light wine and a bird. Despite his insistence that he no longer drank to excess, he might be bloating on ale, or washing a joint down with brandy to a degree that would render him unsteady in the saddle. She would laugh if that had happened, for it would prove that all his fine talk of sobriety was another lie.

Or perhaps, said a small voice at the back of her mind, *he does not wish to be with you.*

That should make her happy, just as the thought of his drunkenness did. If she was riding like a princess, and he was willing to forgo luxury after only two days of marriage to keep apart from her, then she was succeeding in her plan to make him unhappy.

She had never meant to be the sort of person that could not be abided by others. When one was a servant, one could not afford to be disagreeable. Her maid seemed to like her and chattered endlessly as they travelled about the sights they passed. The drivers, grooms and outriders treated her with kindness, as well. They all grinned, rushing over each other for the chance to serve the new duchess, plying her with treats and cushions as though she was fragile as a quail's egg, to be packed in cotton wool and not to be jostled. She had been kind and polite to all of them in return, apologising for any trouble she caused and showing appreciation for their extra efforts.

She'd offered none of that kindness to her husband, who had been willing to sleep in a chair to assure himself that her dreams remained sweet. Of course, her rest would be easier had she never met him....

Try as she might to remind herself that she was justified in her anger with him, she could feel those little moments of sympathy sneaking in, nibbling away like mice in the wainscoting. With comfort and condiments and kindness, he was trying to make amends for what he had done.

And she remembered the look on his face that morning, before he'd turned and ridden away. *I will not let it affect me in front of others. But see what you have forced me to do.*

Yesterday, he had requested her company for that ridiculous trip to Tattersall's and dinner, as well. Today, he did not seem to be bothered by holding apart from her. She had seen him smiling and chatting to the grooms before they'd set off. The few glimpses she'd got of him, when he'd been close enough to the carriage to see, he'd seemed quite content with both his method of transportation and the pace he'd set for himself.

It was only when he'd turned to her that a cloud had passed over his features. And that, only when there was no one else around who might see. As long as he kept away from her, he seemed his usual cheerful self.

It was possible that by tomorrow, she would not see him at all. He would settle her in his county seat and then disappear from her life. He would have all of the rest of England to be happy in. And she would have whatever ground she trod on to be bitter and miserable, even in the face of comfort that should have made a poor little governess jump for joy.

Without logic, the hurt she caused seemed to rebound on her. After she had lost Richard, she had understood that her chance for true happiness had passed. She would be alone until she died. To pass the years, she would keep busy and do good works. Her life would be solitary, but not empty. She had never imagined herself as abandoned, or avoided, until she had married the duke. But now she could picture her future as a very comfortable void.

They stopped again in midafternoon, in a spot just as green and beautiful as the place where she had taken lunch. At supper, they found an inn where she was rushed to a private sitting room, and offered the best that the humble place could offer. The innkeeper and his daughter were scraping and bowing, as though her presence was their greatest possible honour.

She thought to ask whether they had met the duke. Surely they must have, for it seemed this was a regular stop on the way to the manor and the most logical place to sup.

At mention of her husband, the man grinned as though it were possible to see such a great man as friend, pronouncing him kind, gallant and good-humoured.

His daughter produced what was quite obviously a virginal blush and sighed.

So he was a hero in Aldricshire, as well. It was only she who hated him and only she who had been treated with anything less than total respect.

Once again, there was that strange sensation in her stomach. It was probably just the upset of travel against the child forming in her. She had grown used to blaming any discomfort on the baby. But when she analysed the feelings, she was surprised to find that, after a single day of food and sleep, she felt worlds better than she had.

The troubles she was experiencing now were not digestive. They were emotional. Was it envy of the innkeeper and his daughter? Jealousy that they were so obviously happy with the duke? Was this sadness that she was not part of the happy throng surrounding him? He was uniformly kind to friends, servants and strangers, even from the first moment of their acquaintance. But her interactions with him were permanently tainted. And though he gave the same treatment to her, she knew it was given grudgingly.

She had brooded on this for a time, until eventually they arrived at the manor. It was very nearly full dark and the carriage lamps had been lit for some time. But in expectation of their arrival, servants had lit similar lanterns on posts at the sides of the long drive, so that they would know that they were at last home and welcome to be so.

Home. This massive edifice of grey stone was to be her home, for as long as she remained with the duke. Still, there was no sign of the master of the house.

The coachman helped her down and ordered the unloading of her chests. And, when he thought she would not notice, he stepped to the woman waiting at the doorstep and gave her a quick hug and a kiss. Then he was all business again and she was straightening her housekeeper's apron as though wishing to look pin perfect for the new lady of the house.

Maddie shot a quick, questioning look to her maid.

'They are brother and sister,' Peg whispered back. 'But they see each other so rarely, what with her bound to the house here and him being always in London.'

'Surely Blake drives his Grace when he comes home.' Even if he liked to ride, it made no sense that he would not at least send the carriage down as well when he came to Aldricshire.

'But his Grace does not—' Peg stopped as though

unsure how much it was her business to tell, then decided the news must be harmless. 'His Grace rarely stays in the country. He handles as much of the estate business as he can from London and leaves the rest to Mr Upton, who is his manager.'

'But when Parliament is not in session?' Maddie prompted.

'He stays in London.'

'Even in the heat of summer?'

'Sometimes he goes to Bath,' the maid said and then assured her, 'The rooms he has there are quite the finest ones on the Crescent. I am sure, should he take you, that the house he will choose will be even nicer.'

'And at Christmas?' Maddie glanced at the house, imagining it decked with greens and ablaze with lights.

'He is at some house party or other,' the maid said. 'His friends fight for the chance to host him, for he is most diverting company. Many of them have unattached daughters…' The maid realised that she had spoken too freely, to hint to a new bride what a catch her husband had been. 'He always says it would be quite unfair to Mrs Harker to force her to plan entertainments in a house that has no lady, no matter how eager she is to show the dandies from London what true hospitality might look like.' The maid brightened. 'But that will all be changed now you are here.'

Because she was here. Peg was imagining exotic decorations, laughter, music and full guest rooms. For a moment, Maddie was struck by true terror of the change in her position. Arranging for the bridal breakfast had been a lark and she had taken pleasure in planning the most extreme party imaginable.

But it had created an expectation amongst the *ton*. She would be expected to take the reins of a manor and to dress it lavishly, but in good taste. In six months, she would be great with child, or a new mother, and the house would be stacked to the rafters with friends of St Aldric, all expecting her to be the woman who had charmed a duke with her wit and novelty.

If her husband could be forced into her company at all. Which she was beginning to expect he could not.

Then she heard the distant hoofbeats and the trembling in the earth from an approaching horse coming hell for leather up the drive. The black beast seemed to materialise out of the darkness, covering the last yards at a full gallop, only to be brought to a sudden stop in a scattering of stone chips, just in front of the door.

St Aldric came out of the saddle as easily as he had taken it, as though a day's ride ending in a mad dash had been nothing at all to him. As he came forward, he looked at her in the same disapproving, accusatory way he had been doing before turning to look towards the house.

Then she saw the true reason for his displeasure. This time, his expression did not change to his usual benign smile. He glared up at Aldric House—at turrets and wings, at the majestic stone griffons that flanked the entrance and at the perfection of win-

dows, glittering like oil in the darkness about them—
and mere disapproval became loathing.

Perhaps it was a trick of the lantern light. When he
stepped closer to the butler, the housekeeper and the
rest of the waiting servants, his usual grin returned.
It seemed so sincere most times. But it was nothing
more than a role he was used to playing. He seemed
truly to enjoy the company of his servants, enquiring after their health and their children and agreeing
that it was, indeed, a very long time since he had seen
them all. When he chanced to look away from their
faces and at the house he was to enter, there was a
tightness to his smile and a darkness in his blue eyes.

He might like the people and hold a diplomatic dislike for her. But was she the only one to see the truth?
He hated every last stone of his family home.

Chapter Seven

He was home.

Or so the servants thought, at least. Michael was in no mood to enjoy their eager greetings and their good humour about the visit. He had been forced into this. It was yet another punishment for the mistake in Dover and for underestimating the damage he had done to the woman at his side.

Perhaps he deserved to suffer. But it was too much to expect him to enjoy it. When they were through the doors, Madeline was given the briefest possible introduction to the assembled staff. Then he announced that they were 'ready to retire'.

He saw her glancing around at the inlaid marble floor of the entry, the paintings, the mirrors and the width and length of corridors that led off to an impressive number of well-appointed receiving rooms. When she saw the extent of her new home, she would gawk at it like a housemaid on a tour of Chatsworth. If he was kind to her, he'd admit that it was a common response. Even the most jaded aristocrats could not manage to be blasé about Aldric House.

Only one who had lived here could learn to hate it.

The worst was yet to come. He turned to the housekeeper. 'I trust the rooms above are prepared for us?'

She smiled sympathetically back at him. 'They have been opened and aired, but are just as they were left, your Grace.'

'I see.' He had done nothing with the floor above since his parents had died. The memories were too painful. In marrying Evelyn or someone like her, he'd hoped that he might have found a woman capable of taking on the job of renovation. But the wife he had chosen, though she seemed to enjoy spending his money, would likely think the arrangement a fitting punishment and refuse to touch a thing.

He stared down at her, not bothering to disguise his feelings for her, or the situation she had landed him in. 'It is late. Please allow me to show you to your chambers.' Then he set out for the first floor, not bothering to see if she followed.

The last thing he wished was to give further evidence of the man who dragged his heels on these trips and avoided his bed, drinking too long in the library and sleeping before the fire then staggering to his bed only when he was too tired to care. She would confuse weakness for debauchery and think it further evidence of his base character.

He had dodged the trip in a closed carriage, the awkward questions, and even more awkward silences.

He had dawdled along the way and been forced to gallop the last miles to avoid arriving so very much later than the new duchess. In truth, the burst of speed at the end had made it easier. The feeling of the wind in his face was like a cold slap, temporarily banishing imagined demons.

Now he continued the speed and heard her laboured breathing. Judging by the cadence of her heels, she had to take two steps for each one of his. 'You do not have to bother, if you do not wish to,' she said, scampering on the mahogany steps as she hurried to catch up. But he refused to slow for her.

'You were the one who was not content in London.' They had reached the upper hall and he wheeled on her, causing her to draw up short and run into his body. Without thinking, he reached to steady her, then damned himself for his weakness and damned himself again for punishing the mother of his child, who must be tired from the ride. Whatever their differences, his feelings for this place were not her fault. Even without her complaints about the town house, he'd have taken her here eventually. One could not avoid one's family seat for ever.

He smiled down at her, hoping that she could feel the irony of it. 'I had thought you would be interested in your new home. It is quite the grandest you are likely to see in all of England, short of the Colton House and the Grand Pavilion.' After her behaviour in London, he expected her to covet it. To put a price tag on it and think of how many gowns the disposal of it might bring her. But there was no disposing of the prime symbol of his dukedom. If it had been possible, he'd have sold the place years ago.

'Of course I am interested,' she said, her voice small. 'But surely the housekeeper might have helped me to my room. You needn't have bothered,' she repeated. Her eyes were large and round in her white face, as though she feared him again and feared being alone above stairs.

He could understand that, at least, even if he could raise no sympathy. 'The housekeeper does not know it as well as I do.' It was only a house to her. Yet each room held a memory to him, especially the suites. 'She may show you the downstairs tomorrow and give you a formal tour of the grounds. But tonight I will show you your sleeping quarters.'

As he watched, she retreated from him, as though she was expecting a cell with a staple for manacles. Did she think this was some sort of prison?

If so, it was not for her.

He gestured to the left wing as they reached the top of the stairs. 'My rooms. You have made it quite clear that you have no interest in them, so a tour is hardly necessary.'

Then he gestured before him to the darkened alcove at the head of the stairs. 'Behind that door is the nursery wing. There is a schoolroom, a playroom, rooms for children and bedrooms for nurse and governess or tutor. I doubt they have been aired. We will not bother with them tonight.'

He had no doubt that the rooms were not just aired, but immaculate. His staff would allow nothing less. If there was a rumour that the new duchess might be *enceinte*, there would be fresh flowers, fires laid and candles lit tonight, so that the young couple could dote on the future.

The thought made him sick. Better to bring a child up in his bachelor's quarters in Bath than to keep the poor thing here. He tested the door to make sure it was properly locked.

He turned from it and gave a casual gesture to his right. 'These are your rooms. Lest you fear otherwise, this is the last time I will pass through this door.' The hall was not precisely gloomy, but it was long enough that the ensconced candles had to struggle to fight back the darkness.

She peered down the corridor as though afraid to advance.

'Which ones?'

'Why, all of them, of course.' It gave him a small, bitter feeling of satisfaction to see the shock on her face. 'If you wished to sleep apart from me, then your wish is granted.' He pushed open doors as he passed them, barely looking at the interiors. 'Rooms for your maids here and here. There is another closer to the bedroom, so that there will be no delay should you wish to summon her at night.'

'Maids?' The plural surprised her. Very good. The shock was satisfying. Let her see what it truly meant to be the Duchess of St Aldric.

She was staring into the tiny rooms as though any one of them would content her.

'The first guest room.' Far from the duchess, his mother had reserved that as a sort of punishment for those swains who had fallen out of favour.

'The box room for the trunks that will hold your wardrobe, when you travel. It saves the time of the servants hauling the things down from the attic whenever you take a whim to go to London.' It had been another guest room, at one time, before his parents had ceased entertaining in a normal way. He could see Madeline wondering at it. Let the question answer itself. They had reached the end of the main hall and he pushed open doors on either side. 'The guest suites, here, here and here. Each has a dressing room with space for a servant's cot, should they wish to keep valets handy.'

'Or maids,' she added, naive creature that she was.

He led her through the guest room on the left, opening a door on the far wall. 'And here is your salon.'

She was staring into the room, slack jawed with amazement. It had been long enough since he'd seen the room that he felt much the same. While the guest rooms had been similar in design to the elegant rooms of his town house, the salon walls were hung with Oriental silks. A large fireplace warmed it. The crystal chandeliers and sconces were fully lit and sparkling. A dining table and chairs took the middle of the room. At the end, there were armchairs, and in a place of honour, a *chaise longue*, covered in the same decadent fabric as the walls. He pushed through another door behind it to show her the dressing rooms and the maid's cot. 'And here is the corridor that leads to your bedroom.'

If the salon had surprised her, the bedroom left her mute with shock. The exotic decor carried into the bedchamber, with thick rugs from Persia and a floor and bed strewn with cushions. Michael had often thanked God that, as a child, he had been barred from the wing. It saved him the pain of imagining his mother in residence here.

Instead, he glanced down at his petite wife and wondered if she understood the meaning of what she was seeing. 'Do you find this sufficiently remote?'

'It's huge.' She could not manage anything else.

'It is yours,' he said, in blunt response to her amazement. 'There are any number of doors between your room and mine. Each one has a lock, with only a single set of keys. You may open or close doors between the guest rooms and yours as you choose and entertain without fear of interruption. Do with it as you will. Take chocolate, or breakfast in bed. Have suppers in the salon. Entertain here any guests you choose, male or female. It does not matter to the staff, any more than it would to me. This is your sanctum: your refuge from the obviously onerous task of being my wife. It is fully equipped so that you needn't come downstairs at all. Now, if you will excuse me...'

He did not wait for an answer. Instead, he exited through the door on the far wall, which led him into another embarrassingly convenient guest suite, and eventually back into the main hall.

Then he went back towards the master wing, disgusted with his own behaviour. It had given him a sort of sick pleasure to see Madeline stunned to silence by the opulence of her surroundings. But in this house, what other kind of pleasure could there ever be but an unhealthy one? With her trunks full of satins, and her horrible screeching birds and sad wastes of horseflesh, she had thought it possible that he could be shamed, or shocked, or even annoyed. What a silly little girl she was.

It was a pity she had not met his mother. The woman had been a master of that game even before little Madeline was born. And that, too, had been in response to a husband who had earned his punishment.

As he passed the nursery wing, his steps dragged a little. Was it still so cold there, as he remembered it? Now was not the time to investigate, if he wanted an untroubled night's sleep. It would be difficult enough to get any rest here without brandy as an anaesthetic.

Crossing the threshold on his side of the house was almost as difficult as coming to the house in the first place. Card rooms, billiards and a smoking room, all quite nice, if a bit gaudy. But they belonged on the ground floor and not tucked in amongst the bedrooms. Then there were the guest rooms. The staff had not bothered with the candles there, knowing how he detested the sight of their tasteless design. He had seen brothels in London with less of a sense of debauchery than the red-velvet hangings and excessive mirrors of his father's guest chambers.

At least his father had not bothered with the labyrinth of connecting rooms. While his mother had pretended to have favourites, his father had felt no embarrassment for the comings and goings from his bed. In fact, he often kept his door open to incite jealousy amongst the ladies who visited him. If one wanted his attention while he was occupied with another, she had but to enter the room and join in the fun.

Michael paused at the last door before his room, remembering the sly smiles of the women he'd seen leaving this wing, the sudden raucous laughter, smothered whispers and the cries of delight. It had been a stark contrast to the dead silence of his mother's side of the house and the equally silent nursery wing.

When he had been old enough to understand, he'd sworn that his life would never come to this. His behaviour would be exemplary. His marriage would be one of mutual respect. His family would be large and happy.

He had failed. For all the trying to be otherwise, he was his father's son. He went into his father's room, slammed the door and rang for brandy.

Chapter Eight

'But, your Grace, it is so lovely that it would be a shame not to try it.'

Maddie glanced at herself in the mirror, shocked at her appearance. Perhaps there was something in the air of this building that changed one to suit the surroundings. If so, they must open the windows and clear the miasma away. She had gone to sleep in a bedroom suited to a harem. Now her maid was trying to force her into a day dress suitable for a sultan's captive.

'Surely there must be something more practical that would serve.' The ladies she had seen in dishabille at the houses where she'd worked had been far more sensible in their dress. And likely they had been warmer. They'd had the sense to keep their bosoms covered. This confection of ruffles and muslin barely covered hers.

'But it is so very French, your Grace. And you look lovely in it.'

'It does not fit,' she argued. Had it been so terribly low when she'd tried it at the modiste's? Or was it just the pregnancy that had increased what the bodice was supposed to hide? Her breasts seemed to float on a tide of lace, ready to bob to the surface at any moment.

'Do not tug on it, your Grace. You will tear the trim. That is how it is meant to look.'

'I seriously doubt so.' In the mirror, she could see the tops of her nipples peeking over the edge of the neckline. The fabric under it was so sheer that even with lining it hid nothing. But to put on stays and petticoat rather defeated the purpose of dressing for morning comfort.

'Perhaps just a touch of rouge,' the maid suggested, glancing at her décolletage.

Maddie did not need rouge to create a flush in her nipples or anywhere else. The idea was completely scandalous and the blush it created was natural.

'It is only to take chocolate in the salon,' her maid prompted. 'No one need ever see.'

She wanted to argue that that alone was reason not to bother with it. But the sumptuousness of her surroundings seemed to call for such behaviour. The memory of the satin coverlet against her cheek and the ridiculously large bed that practically screamed to be sported in...

This was the true danger of her long-ago fall from grace. She knew too much about such things. Although the memory of Richard grew dimmer with each passing day, the sight of her husband's bare flank was etched for ever in memory. She could imagine running her hand along that flesh, the way he might respond to it and the feelings of pleasure that would arise in her to see him aroused.

The room felt unaccountably hot as she thought of it.

The past two weeks had been spent in a panicked rush towards the performance of wedding and breakfast. This morning would be the first uninterrupted quiet she'd had in ages. But that did not mean that she must sit barely dressed on a satin cushion, thinking scandalous thoughts about St Aldric's legs. It would have been more in character to find a book and a quiet spot to enjoy it in.

But that would have required roaming this museum of a house for a library. If the ground floor was anything like the bedrooms, there was no telling what disasters might await her. With its maze of connected rooms, her wing seemed designed to separate her from the rest of the world. Was she to be a prisoner here? Was it a punishment? Or did he truly think that such total privacy was either necessary or welcome?

It was quite beyond comprehension until after some sort of breakfast. She gave up with an exasperated sigh. 'Very well, then. I shall wear the gown. But no rouge,' she said hurriedly. 'And I will keep my wrapper handy, should I take a chill. Bring chocolate and some toast. And an egg or two.' She thought again. 'And some of the condiment that St Aldric recommended.' If nothing else, she must thank the man for the return of her appetite.

'Hallo,' a feminine voice called from the next room. 'Is her Grace receiving?'

'Evelyn?' She reached for her robe, but it was too late. The midwife had already entered.

'So this is where you are hiding.' Mrs Hastings poked her smiling head through the connecting doorway of the first guest suite. 'I am unannounced. And for that, I am sorry. Sam is talking with Michael on the opposite side of the house. But they deemed it inappropriate to entertain me in the duke's bedchamber. So I came to seek you out.'

'And I am deporting myself half-naked, like the Queen of Sheba,' Maddie said glumly.

'In this environment, one can hardly blame you,' Evelyn said with sympathy. 'If it helps you to know it, the downstairs is quite normal.'

'That is a relief. I had not seen it yet and feared the worst. When we arrived, St Aldric escorted me directly to this wing and abandoned me.'

Eve glanced around her at the opulent hangings. 'It is rather much, is it not? The dowager had passed long before my visit to Aldricshire. Michael took me no farther than the dower house and the receiving rooms downstairs. But if this room is any indication, his mother must have been quite colourful.'

'That is a charitable description at best.'

Evelyn admired her costume. 'And I must say that your current attire suits the room well. It is very…'

'Wanton?' Maddie asked, staring down at her own breasts.

'I was going to say feminine,' Evelyn supplied.

'I look like a Cyprian,' she said, tugging at her bodice again.

'I have seen more shocking sights in London, I am sure. It is a very pretty gown. In the privacy of your own home, it will do no harm. And Michael will find it most fetching.'

Michael again. Though Maddie could not manage it, Evelyn had no trouble calling the duke by his Christian name. Michael had brought Evelyn to Aldricshire. And apparently, it had been without her husband. It all sounded very cosy.

'I do not care if my husband appreciates the style,' Maddie said, annoyed. 'He will not find me on a recamier with my gown half falling off.'

Evelyn came to sit at her side and took her hand. 'I did not mean to tease you so. You may change if you like. But I think you are lovely, just as you are.'

'Thank you,' she said with relief. 'But the room is terrible, is it not? I think it is affecting my mood.'

Evelyn nodded in sympathy.

'And you say you have been here before?' She paused for a moment to give Eve a chance to correct her understanding, and added, 'With your husband, of course. He must know the estate well.'

Evelyn paused. 'Actually, he has never seen the place. Nor did he meet his father.' She paused again.

'How much has Michael told you of our history to-gether?'

There was the name again. And the implication that this woman knew much more about her husband than she did herself. Did he mean to keep secrets from her? Or had he not thought it worth the effort to share them? 'Absolutely nothing,' Maddie admitted at last. Then she added, 'You know much more of my past than I do of yours.' Not that there was likely to be anything exceptionable about Evelyn. She seemed the epitome of social grace and decorum.

But Evelyn sighed as though relieved to unburden herself. 'It was not too many months ago that we all assumed I would be the Duchess of St Aldric. I was engaged to Michael. For less than a week,' she added hurriedly. 'But we courted for most of the Season and there was an expectation.'

How horrible. 'And then he…'

Evelyn laughed. 'No, darling. It had nothing to do with you at all.' She sobered and said, in a small voice, 'But I fear that I might have had some part in what occurred in Dover. It was after the broken engagement, you see, that Michael ran amok. It was the illness as well, of course. But it was also about that time that I chose his brother instead of him. And though he claimed that he was not bothered, I worried.'

'Because you had affection for him?'

'As a brother. Nothing more than that.' Evelyn looked relieved to be able to tell the story. 'There was never anyone for me but Sam. I have known him for as long as I can remember and loved him almost as long. But he was far from London and had never met Michael. And when I did…' She gave a helpless shrug and smiled. 'You must see the resemblance. I had to bring the two together. So I cultivated Michael's interest, persuaded Sam to return to London, the two of them were introduced and learned the truth….' She shrugged again. 'It was all a bit of a muddle, for a time. But things worked out for the best. We are quite happy now. And you will be, as well. Despite his behaviour when you met him, Michael truly is a saint amongst men, though he hates to admit. He will be a wonderful father and a husband, as well.'

'And now we are all in Aldricshire together,' Maddie added. Once again, she was the interloper, just as she had been in London.

'Sam is the duke's personal physician,' Eve explained. 'Not that his services are required, of course. Michael is as healthy as an ox. But we will admit to some curiosity about the house and grounds. Sam knows practically nothing of his father. And Michael rarely speaks of his childhood and visits the house even less so.' Evelyn smiled and laid a finger on the side of her nose. 'So I proclaimed it my professional opinion that you could not possibly manage without a midwife, so that we might use your strategic retreat to the country to investigate. I hope you do not mind.'

It was too late to object, even if she did. 'Of course not. But I know little about the place myself and I am not sure where best to put you.'

'It is all arranged,' Evelyn assured her. 'Michael suggested the dower house and it is quite suitable for our needs. It is small and utterly charming, tastefully decorated and far enough away so that you might have the privacy you need.'

Evelyn seemed to imagine a happy honeymoon already in progress. It was just another sign of the woman's optimism. 'We have too much privacy already. This whole wing is mine to command. The duke has space of his own on the opposite side of the house.'

By the worried look on Evelyn's face, the arrangement was as odd as it appeared. 'The estrangement between the last duke and duchess must have been more deep than Michael let on. Sam was born shortly after Michael. The duke never acknowledged him. The duchess was upset. This—' she waved a hand to encompass the house '—must have been the result.'

And now the new duke had married a near stranger who had requested a divide between them as deep or deeper than any his parents had known. The experience must be quite painful for him.

But had that not been the object all along? If she meant to hurt him, she had succeeded in making him come here. But strangely, there was no joy in it.

'It must have been difficult for him,' Maddie said cautiously. 'He does not seem to like the place at all. If mine are any indication, I cannot imagine what his rooms must look like.'

'So Michael is sequestered on the other side of the

house and you have not seen his rooms?' Eve raised her eyebrows.

'We have only just arrived,' Maddie said hurriedly, not wanting the situation to sound any more unusual than it already was.

'Well, I am aflame with curiosity. I will torment Sam mercilessly until he has uncovered every last detail. Then I shall share them with you.'

'Please, don't.' Even in war, there must be some rules. And if anything were hallowed ground, it should be childhood.

'It is all right, I am sure,' Evelyn announced, paying no attention. 'If he thought to marry me, he must have known that I would learn all his secrets.'

'As if I could manage to keep anything from you, Evelyn. You are a terrible nuisance and I am lucky to be rid of you.' The duke entered, his tone affectionate and his attention focused on his former fiancée.

Then he froze in the doorway, shocked to immobility. He was staring at Maddie, half-clothed and reclining, just as she had feared he would. His gaze was riveted to the neckline of her gown and the non-existent coverage it provided her modesty. His blue eyes were practically black. His breathing was slow, deep and, without thinking, hers slowed to match it. The air between them seemed to crackle with tension. Her nipples tightened as though presenting themselves to be kissed.

Deep inside, she felt a trembling, like the rush of water, and the growing desire to relax into it, lean back onto the chaise and show him that the skirt was as thin as the bodice. The muslin would caress her legs and reveal their curves to him. And he would smile and send Evelyn away.

Beside her, she heard Evelyn giggle. Then the duke broke his gaze and turned to speak to someone in the hall behind him.

Sam Hastings. Evelyn would not be laughing if her own husband entered the room to find her in this condition. The man was a physician. But that did not mean she wished to be displayed before him like an anatomy lesson. Maddie grabbed for the blue wool wrapper and shrugged into it, pulling it tight over breasts and thighs to hide her shame.

'And here you both are at last,' Evelyn said, ignoring her scramble for decency. 'Michael, you must take us all through the public rooms. The tour you gave me last year was most interesting. Maddie must be eager to see her new home.'

'I am sure she is,' St Aldric said. He was staring carefully into her eyes, as though the interlude a moment ago had never happened.

'Well, she must not set out without a guide,' Sam announced, entering the room, oblivious to what had just occurred. 'If the rest of the house is as confusing as this wing, we shan't see her again if we leave her to find her own way.'

'I am sure she will be fine. Now, come along, the pair of you.' Eve rose and took them both by the arms. 'Take me to the breakfast room, for I am simply famished. Maddie will meet us there directly, when she has dressed.'

As they left, Peg appeared with the forgotten eggs and toast.

Maddie waved it away. 'It seems we are breakfasting below, with the Hastings. Find me a gown I can wear without creating a scandal. Then, for God's sake, find me someone who can show me to the breakfast room.'

After they had eaten, Michael led the little group through the ground floor, reciting what he knew of art and architecture by rote and watching their reactions. They were properly impressed. Madeline, particularly, was in awe. Her soft lips parted in a continual 'oh' of surprise. It was a pity that she had changed the gown, for the thought of those perfect breasts rising and falling with each 'ooh' and 'aah' would have been a beautiful sight.

The appearance of her, careless of her beauty and displayed for him like an Aphrodite in that horrible salon, would cause him many restless nights, he was sure. Judging by the dress she had chosen to replace it, overly heavy, overly drab and covering her practically to the chin, there would be no repeat appearance of the goddess once the guests had gone. It was a pity. For all their difficulties, he could not deny that she was the most human thing in this mausoleum he had inherited and the most beautiful.

For now he contented himself with casting sidelong glances at her and watching her amazement at each new glory: inlaid floors, carpets as thick as fur upon them, white marble fireplaces scrubbed so clean they might never have held an ash, crystal, china and gold. At least there was something she admired about him. If she had meant to spend his purse to empty, she must see how impossible that would be. Mother had tried it upon Father, without success. Madeline would have no better luck with him.

The supper that cook prepared for them was a fitting ending to the day: the best food on the thinnest plates, with the heaviest knives and the whitest linen. And, as he had requested, a tureen of Wow-Wow sauce. Cook had been quietly horrified, thinking it was a reflection on her seasoning. Then he'd made it clear that it was for the duchess, whose digestion, of late, had been delicate. Cook had smiled knowingly and prepared the sauce.

There would be gossip below stairs. But for a change, it would be happy gossip.

Tonight, Evelyn was making enough conversation for the four of them. Michael sometimes found her outspoken nature more annoying than endearing. But it was better than the uneasy silence that he'd have had to endure, had he eaten alone with Madeline.

'I am sure Maddie particularly enjoyed the music room,' Evelyn announced.

'Of course,' he said, wondering if his wife had some talent in that area. He ventured a guess at what might have caught her fancy. 'The harp is particularly lovely. It has been in the family for three generations.'

'The school did not have a harp,' Eve informed him. 'But she is quite proficient on the pianoforte.'

Madeline remained silent.

Was this meant as some sort of hint as to her past? 'You taught it, at this school?' he offered.

'I took lessons,' Madeline replied, still looking down at her plate. 'When I was a student. Before taking work as a governess.'

The conversation was faltering and Evelyn rushed to rescue it. 'It is a shame that the Colvers could not come to the wedding breakfast. I am sure they would have been most proud to see you so well settled.'

Who were these people and how was he expected to know them? He had known his wife only a few weeks and had learned nothing about her past. But in that time, Eve seemed to have gathered a wealth of information.

'I did not think it necessary to inform them. I have not seen them in years,' Madeline said, still not looking up.

Perhaps she had thought he would not allow common folk in his house. If so, it was unfair of her. What difference would a few more guests have made to that bird-infested farce of a breakfast? 'If there was family that you wished to have, we could have arranged it,' he said as patiently as possible.

Madeline raised her eyes and gave him a pointed look. 'They were not my family. They were the people that my true parents paid to keep me until I was old enough to board. Then they washed their hands of me. If they should hear of my rise in station, they will likely appear. But I see no reason to seek them out.'

'Then you are…'

'A bastard,' she informed him.

Why had he even begun the sentence? It was beyond tactless to discuss her parentage at dinner. It displayed his total ignorance of Madeline's past and her feelings about it.

Eve was nodding in satisfaction, as though she had scored a point in a game. If they were playing, she could at least have shared the rules with the rest of them.

Sam seemed very busy with his roasted potatoes and oblivious of the conversation, but then he found it amusing to let his wife run wild and torment the rest of them. Michael ground his teeth and struggled to maintain his composure.

Now that Eve had finished with Madeline, she turned the conversation, indirectly, to Michael.

'As I was saying, the tour of the house was delightful. Especially the bedrooms. They are quite unique. But I based my opinion on the duchess's wing only.' She glanced at her husband. 'I take it Michael showed you his rooms, Sam?'

When addressed directly, Sam could not ignore her. So he nodded and took a large bite of meat, chewing slowly so that he could not answer.

'Well? What were they like?' Evelyn leaned forward to hear the answer.

The doctor swallowed. 'They were...' Sam glanced at Michael, as if wishing to spare him pain.

'As ghastly as the duchess wing?' Eve supplied.

'A bit much to take,' Sam said diplomatically.

'Details please, Dr Hastings,' she said with the impish smile that Michael had found rather irritating when he'd courted her. 'You are a man of science. Do not make diagnoses using such vague words. How did you find the duke's wing?'

'Evelyn.' Michael smothered the anger he was feeling and kept his tone low and cautionary.

Sam gave him another apologetic look, then replied. 'It was a cross between a gaming hell and a house of ill fame.'

'So it was a fitting contrast to the seraglio on the other side of the house.'

Michael threw his napkin aside. 'That is quite enough, the both of you. You come into my house and defame my family—'

'Our family,' Evelyn corrected.

'I beg your pardon?'

'We are in your house because you invited us here. You have encouraged us for some months to treat your properties as our own. Sam is your brother. I am your sister-in-law.' She glanced across the table. 'And Maddie is your wife. Soon, she will be the mother of your child. We are your family, Michael. If there is a burden to bear, who better than us to share it with you?'

'It is not a burden,' he insisted. But if it had not been, why did his heart feel easier now that others had seen it?

'It is an unnecessary secret to the people at this table,' Eve said. 'It is obvious changes will need to be made if you wish to reside here. You could have informed Madeline of the fact rather than dropping her into the middle of it.' Then she turned to Madeline. 'And you, Maddie, might have explained your past to Michael to prevent embarrassment later. Illegitimacy need not be a shameful thing. But openness between the two of you would have prevented the awkward exchange I orchestrated tonight.'

'We hardly know each other,' Madeline argued.

'But you will have a child between you. And while you might go your separate ways later, it is less shocking to claim ignorance of the present behaviour of a spouse than to know nothing of their past.'

Michael glared at her. 'I suppose you mean to give us no peace until you are sure every stone has been turned up and we have no privacy at all?'

Sam sighed, pushing aside his plate. 'I suspect that is true. The woman is relentless, your Grace. I have not had a moment's peace since I married her.'

'And you have never been happier,' Eve informed him.

'Yes, Evie,' he said, and shrugged in defeat. But Michael could tell by the glint in his eye that he was secretly amused. 'Now, if you will excuse us, Michael, I think we will forgo pudding and port and make our way back to the dower house. It is a short walk, but the weather appears to be changing and I do not wish to be caught out in the rain.'

'Very well.' Michael stood and, with his wife, they escorted their guests to the door.

When the other couple had departed, a moment of silence fell between them, as he searched for words. 'I am sorry,' he said. 'For Evelyn.'

'Evelyn is—' Madeline smiled. 'Evelyn is Evelyn. She cannot help but meddle, I think.'

'I am sorry for my own behaviour, as well,' he added. 'I was rude and neglectful of you. I should have asked after your family and your past.'

'There was very little time,' she said, staring out the window over the dark grounds.

'I should have made the time.' Eve had been right. Even if this was not a love match, there should be respect and courtesy on his part. 'There is another wing to view, you know, other than the bedrooms.'

'The nursery?' If she was curious, it did not show.

'Come. We will tour it, then we can retire.' Behind locked doors on opposite ends of the house. No matter how he tried, life here had not changed so very much. But if it was necessary to share secrets with one's wife, the last of them were there.

Chapter Nine

They mounted the stairs and he fished in his pocket for the key. The lock on the door to this wing was unusually heavy. Judging by the slight scratches in the wood and the shininess of the brass compared to the other doors, it was more recently installed. What could be here that needed to be so tightly contained?

'I keep my slaughtered brides in the last room, if that is what you are wondering,' he said with a sigh.

Despite herself, she started.

He sighed again. 'I am not actually Bluebeard, if that is what you suspect. It is just a nursery, as I said yesterday. I keep it locked because...I had no need of it.'

But the strange pause told her there was more to the story.

He had found the correct key, and it turned smoothly in the lock. It was well oiled, as were the hinges of the door. When he crossed the threshold, he shivered. 'It is good that you are dressed warmly.

There is sometimes a chill in this corridor. We will not linger long here.'

It was an odd statement. In a wool coat, he should be warmer than she. Yet she felt no change in temperature. He had taken a taper from the hall and lit candles as they went, opening doors and explaining the rooms and their purposes.

If he had sought her professional opinion as a woman who had seen more than the usual share of nurseries, this one was every bit as splendid as the ground-floor rooms had been. There was none of the ridiculous ostentation of the duchess wing, nor the maze of interconnected rooms. The nursery wing was laid out quite sensibly. The main room was more pleasant than any she had worked in. In daytime, light would shine through the mullioned windows. She was sure, when she opened them, she would feel a fresh breeze and hear the faint sound of the river a few miles away.

The room would serve as a sitting room for the children and their teacher. She could see the varying doors leading from it lead to a schoolroom, a suite of bedrooms for older children and a proper nursery with cradle for little ones. The last door she opened led to a bedroom and sitting room for the governess.

She could not help the little thrill of satisfaction she felt at the sight of it. It was well appointed and cheerful, and much nicer than anything she might have expected from her last posting. This was the sort of place that suited her, not the grand room of a duchess.

She fought to control the smile as she turned back to him. She was not brought here to tend the children. He would think her quite mad if she requested to move her things to this bedroom. No matter how preferable it might be, it was not meant for her.

The duke stood, his back to her, staring out the window into the darkness. Lightning flashed in the distance and the first streaks of rain marred the glass. 'As you can see, it is quite grim here. I would be obliged if you devoted some portion of your time to have it properly equipped for the child. You have some professional knowledge of such places after all.'

'Grim?' she said, surprised. That was the last word she'd have used for the shelves of books and the cupboard that must be full of playthings.

He nodded, still not turning. 'I have not been here in quite some time. I had hoped it had changed. But unfortunately, no. This room is exactly as I remember it. Strip it to the bare walls and start again.'

She had thought to spend his money like water out of spite. But every fibre in her resisted making changes to a setting so perfect for the raising of children. She imagined her own child here and felt the little stirrings of excitement in her heart at the thought of a baby of her own. It would be St Aldric's child, of course. And he would be possessive of the heir and the law was quite clear on his ownership.

But by nourishing it with her heart's blood, and keeping it safe in her belly, it was hers, as well. Despite what Eve had said in the dining room. It would be her first true family.

But this room called to hold a large and happy brood, not just the only baby they were to have together.

'So much space for one child.' She imagined the neat rows of beds in the school that had housed her. She'd had not a moment's peace until she'd left it. She had longed for privacy. But as the only child in this monstrous house, he would have been lonely. She felt an unbidden sympathy for the man.

He did not turn. 'There were nurses, of course. Teachers. A governess or two.'

'Did you enjoy their company?' The children she'd watched had grown quite fond of her.

'Father chose them and discarded them according to their education and my needs.' He described them as though they were so many possessions. But for a twist of fate, he might have thought the same of her.

She turned to the cupboard to see what it was that the young marquis had entertained himself with. The shelves were surprisingly empty. She had expected blocks, puzzles, balls and lead soldiers. Instead she saw row upon row of carefully aligned models. She took one up: a tiny sheep with real wool and four dark legs that were little more than twists of wire. Behind it was a fishing boat with full crew and nets made of thread full of tiny lead fish. After that came houses, farms, shops and mats of straw painted like water, crops and roads.

'This was yours?' It was surprising. Knowing children as she did, she'd never have trusted them with something so delicate and so obviously valuable.

'And my father's before me.' He had come to stand beside her, taking up a tiny farmer and turning it in his hands. 'Each little figure was modelled on an actual tenant. The houses you see here in miniature still stand on the roads.'

'You played with real people?' It was strange and barbaric to think of a little boy playing God over this tiny world.

'Of course not.' He shuddered again and placed the figure carefully on the shelf. 'I learned from them. I knew names, places, each brick in the road and each sheep in the field.'

'If they broke, were you punished for it?'

'They did not break,' he said. 'I saw to that. If they were damaged, I mended them. If they wanted paint, I took up the brush and did it myself. They are as clean and perfect as the day they were made.'

But he did not seem happy about it. His usual, somewhat artificial, smile had become something much more grim.

'Will your son play with them, as well?'

He hesitated. And since he rarely did, the pause was profound. 'It is an excellent way to learn one's holdings.'

'But it is a great responsibility for a small child.' She picked up the sheep again and touched one of the legs, giving it a gentle push with her fingertip, seeing the wire bend.

The man beside her was holding his breath. She was sure, if she went so far as to break the little animal, he would feel his own leg snap.

She released the pressure and set it gently back on the shelf. 'It is very interesting. But I see no reason to keep the wing locked. Or to have a lock on the door at all. Why did you bother to seal it up?'

'Why did I install a lock?' He laughed. 'My parents did that when I was still young to keep me from roaming the house.'

'Your parents locked you in.' The idea was unfathomable. She had been in strict households, of course. And dealt with undisciplined children. But never had there been the need to keep them prisoner. It was beyond imaging that the little boy who had cared for toy people as though they were real could cause enough trouble to need a lock on his door.

'I was too curious,' he said with a shrug. 'My parents had little time for me. I had the run of the house and grounds when they were in London. But when they were here, they retired to their wings with their friends and did not wish to be bothered.' He reached to straighten one of the toy buildings and returned the sheep she had examined to what must have been its proper place.

'Sam was concerned that his birth had caused the estrangement between them,' he said, 'but I am sure it was far deeper than that. It was my birth that gave them the excuse to lead separate lives. Once they had an heir, they did not need each other.'

Apparently they had not needed him either. 'It must have been very lonely for you to be shut up here, away from everything.'

'I thought so, at first,' he said. 'Until they locked the door, I would creep about the house at night, trying to discover what it was that so fascinated them.'

'And what did you find?' She could guess the answer.

'Not my parents, that is for certain. My mother kept her doors locked, long before they closed up the nursery. But my father's wing was open. And there was a woman there who offered to explain everything to me.' He shut the cupboard door, but did not look at her as he spoke. 'I suspect she was angry at having to share my father's attentions. Or perhaps she was jealous that her husband was with my mother. She said she would show me everything. So I followed her into one of the bedrooms and had my answer.'

'While you were still in the nursery?' Surely he would have gone away to school when he was old enough. But that meant he was... 'Just how old were you?'

'I don't remember,' he said firmly, as though he did not like to look too closely at the past. 'But not more than twelve. She said there would be cake after.' He smiled, as though it were a joke. 'I remember it was a deciding factor.' He paused. 'To this day, I cannot abide sweets. And I cannot stand this house. But perhaps now you understand how I came to be the sort of man who might attack governesses. For all I know, it is a family trait. Now, if you will excuse me, I am tired.' He fished in his pocket and handed her the keys to the nursery. 'Put out the candles and lock the door when you leave.'

Then he turned and left her in the most silent wing of the house.

Chapter Ten

The storm that had been just a threat during supper had finally broken and was hammering the windows. Maddie slid down under the covers, waiting for it to end. It was unusual that rain bothered her. When dealing with children, it had been her job to provide the comfort. But this house was so very strange. She had been too tired to notice it last night. But tonight, after talking to the duke, she felt it in her bones. To be the only person in a wing made her feel all the more isolated.

And to do that to a child…

Even with governesses and teachers and nurses, and the fact that the surroundings were far from appropriate, a child would want to see his parents. It sometimes seemed that the less interested the parents were, the more the little ones craved attention. They must have thought they were protecting him by keeping him isolated. It had come too late, of course. The story he'd told had been quite horrible. He had been far too young to understand what was happening to him.

· When she had come to London, St Aldric had seemed so far beyond the reach of ordinary humans that she could hardly comprehend. The world bowed to his title and thought him a saint. And in her mind, he had been by parts a villain and a sham.

She had never expected to find him so human once all artifice had been stripped away. To see the house, and his reaction to it, she could imagine the frightened little boy he had been. His parents had not known what to do with him and had locked him away. And so he had retreated into his toy fiefdom to become the man his father had not been.

He had been wrong. The nursery had been warm enough. But the bed she was lying in was large and cold, and she hated it. If she stayed here, was she destined to become as his mother had been, entertaining favourites in secret and keeping her child behind a locked door? At one time, she might have thought it a fit punishment for St Aldric. But no matter the past, she would not stoop so low. Whatever else she might say of him, the duke did not want to turn his back on his offspring as his parents had done to him. Or as hers had done to her.

There was much that she did not understand about the Duke of St Aldric. But she was sure of one thing: he had been lonely here. Likely, he still was. A person with many true friends did not need to be as polite and guarded as he had become. At supper tonight, Evelyn had needed to remind him that he had any family at all. If this was how he behaved with those nearest and dearest to him, she doubted that anyone in England was acquainted with the real Michael Poole hiding behind the saintly title.

He had no one and neither did she.

If Madeline understood anything, it was loneliness. And tonight she did not want to be alone. Though they were joined in matrimony, they were separated by class, by circumstance and by the width of this enormous house. Perhaps they were too different to be one in spirit. But there was another, very physical way to ease the pain of isolation.

She had meant to keep apart from St Aldric, fearing him and her uncontrollable response to him in Dover. But why? She was no longer some shy governess protecting what was left of her reputation. She had survived ruin not just once but twice. And while chastity might be sensible for a spinster, in a married woman it was unnatural.

She could remember the way the duke had looked at her this morning when he had surprised her in the salon. He had wanted her. And her body had responded. The feeling was still there, and building in her. Her breasts were tender with it. Her body throbbed. Her mind was alert to the presence of him, lying alone somewhere on the other side of the house.

Lightning flashed again, with thunder following close upon it. It gave her a brief view of gold tassels and silk draperies, etched in sharp relief before the darkness came again. It was a crime to find such ugliness in a house that should be so beautiful. And judging by Sam's description, the duke's room was no better.

Perhaps St Aldric had told the truth when he said he had changed for the better. He seemed a different man from the one she had met in the inn. But he was different from the one she had married in London, as well. His quick wit and false smile failed him here. He was unhappy. He was vulnerable. And she was no longer afraid of him.

She pulled her nightgown over her head and dropped it, ignored her sensible robe and pulled the sheet from her bed, wrapping it around her body to keep away the chill.

Then she took the winding way through her suite to the main hall and the door at the end of it. A few more steps and she was standing at the door to his wing. It would not be locked, she was sure. He'd had enough of locked doors. She was right. The knob turned without resistance, and the hinges were as silent as the nursery door.

Beyond it, the hall was dark but for a pair of sconces at the end. It was a relief, for she was sure she did not want to see the details. It was enough to know that the rugs muffled her footsteps and the mirrors on the walls showed her the golden glow of candlelight on her own flesh. She reached out to trace her fingers along the wall and touched not paper, but velvet. Thick fabric curtains deadened sound and concealed

God knew what sins. There was a heaviness in the air, as well. Incense? Tobacco? Or was it opium? It made her feel light-headed. Perhaps that was just nerves.

Unlike her own wing, there was a door at the very end of this hall. It was the logical place for the master's room. Her hand paused on that doorknob for a moment, then turned it and pushed the door open. She went through, closing it behind her, and was plunged into immediate darkness.

But she did not need sight to know that she had found him. While the hall might smell of sin, this room smelled of him. Cologne and musk, brandy and tobacco. She had noticed it earlier as they'd stood together in the nursery. There it had been reassuring. Now her body gave an answering shudder as it sensed he was near.

The fire had died in the grate, but another flash of lightning showed her the figure on the bed. He was lying on his back, a hand across his eyes. The sheet that should have covered him was tossed aside, revealing his naked body to her for the first time. The light was gone again. But she did not need it to remember what she had seen. The strong limbs, the broad shoulders and chest tapering to a narrow waist and the powerful manhood that would wake to her touch.

She surrendered to her desire and climbed into his bed.

He woke with a start and tried to sit up.

She pushed him back down with a hand on the middle of his bare chest and he relaxed as he recognised her, waiting for her to speak. 'You said I could have what I wanted,' she said. 'And tonight, I want this.' Then she reached between his legs and stroked him once, from root to tip.

The body that had been sleeping came instantly alive and she felt another answering shudder inside of her as she coaxed him to full erection.

For a moment, he seemed too shocked to move. Then his hand closed over hers, stroking once with it before pulling it away to twine his fingers with hers. He pulled her forward onto his body so that she could lie atop him, chest to breast and leg over leg.

And when their lips met, she knew she had been right in coming here. The kiss was gentle, but only for a moment. Then it dissolved into a thing of mutual hunger, open mouthed and desperate. Had she forgotten so much? Or had she never been kissed like this? His lips were sweet and she could not get enough of them. His tongue delved deep and then swirled against her lips before he withdrew to suck and bite his way down her neck to her breast.

Nothing had ever felt this good. They had barely begun and she could already feel the first tremors of orgasm. But before she was finished, she wanted to touch every inch of him and feel him moving inside her.

She pulled away from him and he moaned at the loss, reaching for her to bring her close again. She laughed and batted his hands away, then dipped her fingers in the moisture pooling between her own legs and spread it on him. And then she rose up on her knees and teased herself with the tip of him, spreading herself, working him against the little nub there for a moment before sliding down to sheathe him with her body.

There was another bolt of lightning and she saw him smile. Perhaps it was the stark-white light that seemed to change his features, but the look on his face was different from his drawing room expression. He was staring up at her with pure, unguarded joy. Even if it only lasted for a moment, she was lying with the man and not the title. Her body responded with a shudder of delight.

The storm broke as they moved together, accompanied by the rumble of thunder. Flashes of brilliant white light gave her brief glimpses of his arched throat and his hands reaching for her, just before they settled between her legs. His fingers spanned the crease at the top of her thighs and his thumbs joined to rub circles against her.

As his tempo increased, her control slipped and she leaned forward, grasped his biceps and thrust against him, faster and faster, crying out as she felt him spend himself inside of her, letting it carry her over the edge.

She collapsed against him, exhausted. He pulled her close, burying his face in her hair and brushing the loose strands of it together with his hands. Neither of them spoke and she was glad of it. She did not want to explain to him why she was with him. She was not sure she had an answer for it. She only knew that it been good. The storm was passing. She was at peace now and he was beginning to doze, so she kissed him one last time upon the forehead and fumbled for the sheet. She wrapped it around her body and crept back down the hall to her own room and bed.

What had just happened?

Michael lay flat on the mattress just as she had left him, trying to analyse the situation. He was cold. His bed sheet was missing. It was proof that what he'd experienced was not just some erotic dream.

When he stumbled across the room to stoke the fire, he found the sheet she had been wearing when she'd come to him. It smelled of perfume and musk. He gathered it to his face and inhaled deeply before taking it back to bed.

The day had been full of unexpected events. The arrival of the Hastingses had given him the chance to explain some of the more embarrassing family history to Sam. His brother had taken the news as he took all surprises, with the calm measured response of a physician. It had put Michael at ease.

And then to find Madeline wearing that gown… Common sense should have made him insist that she cover herself in the presence of guests. Instead, his mouth had watered at the sight of her. Her breasts were full, ripe and barely covered. He had wanted nothing more in that moment than to send the guests away, lean her back on the chaise and bury his face in them. He had not wanted to acknowledge an attraction for her, but it was there. And it was growing stronger.

Had she known what his response would be? Did she come to him because she felt something, as well? Or was this meant as some new torture?

Perhaps he had married a succubus. She had taken something from him, and it was more than just a bed sheet. It felt as though some substantial part of him had gone missing after the brief exchange between them. If the soul had been a corporeal thing, something that he could lay hands upon and test for soundness, he'd have done it now. Had she stolen it?

He thought not. He was lighter, but in no way incomplete. He felt drained, but giddy. If he looked into the mirror, he would likely be smiling. If she was trying to hurt him, then she truly did not understand men. It had been the excitement of an anonymous encounter that had got him into this situation. And he had thought those days were behind him.

It had never occurred to him that one might find such bliss with one's own wife. They might not find common ground in daylight, but the occasional erotic encounter in the night would be most welcome. Sam had hinted that some women, when with child, were taken with hysteria that might manifest in this way. He had said that there was no real harm in it. But the advantages were obvious. The only disadvantage Michael could imagine was the chance that, once the child was born, this desire would be a distant memory to her and they would be strangers for the full four-and-twenty hours of the day.

He sobered suddenly. If his life had gone just a hair differently, if he had not taken sick, or at least remained sober in Dover, he might have found a companion for both days and nights.

Then he set the thought aside. He knew little of marriage and even less of love. He had seen successful examples of neither, other than through Sam and Evelyn. But he did understand physical satisfaction, and he had achieved that tonight. He closed his eyes, laid his cheek against the perfumed sheet and slept.

Chapter Eleven

Maddie awoke the next morning with a strange contentment. The bed, which had seemed large and intimidating the night before, was warm and cosy, even though it was empty. It was still too quiet, of course. She wished that the duke occupied a room in this wing so that she might hear the sounds of another human being waking nearby. There should be servants talking, doors opening and closing and perhaps a laugh or a cough.

She buried her face in the sheet she had taken from his room, catching a whiff of his scent. She was not alone. When she had set out on her adventure the previous night, she'd given no thought to what the morrow might bring. But what was she to do now?

Peg was laying out the same dress she'd chosen yesterday, still hoping that Maddie would agree to it. And part of her did. Today, if the duke came to her wing and saw her in it, things might be quite different.

But Sam and Evelyn might arrive again and embarrass her. She waved the gown away and requested something with a higher neck, but without the prudish modesty of the one she'd changed to yesterday. She had not thought herself vain, but she spent an unusual amount of time admiring it in the mirror before declaring it suitable. She wanted to be sure that the colour flattered her and that the bodice showed enough of her blossoming body to attract, but not so much as to give offence.

Only then did she allow Peg to begin upon her hair. In the past, a centre part and a few pins had been enough. But today, she wondered whether curls might not be needed to add softness around her face.

Was she stalling? Or did she seriously want to look her best before meeting the man whose bed she had shared last night?

Either way, Maddie's heart was pounding by the time she walked down to the breakfast room and came face-to-face with the duke.

He smiled as she entered the room, but he always did, even when he was not glad to see her. It was not last night's smile. This was the same sort that he gave to Evelyn. Not exactly insincere, but common. 'Eggs?' he asked. Without waiting for an answer, he took the dish and filled her plate, then pushed the sauce dish in her direction, as well.

'Thank you.' Her response was as empty as his offer. Did he have nothing to say other than to offer her food?

'You're most welcome.' Was that a hint of a real smile she saw on his face? But it was gone, replaced by the same detached look he often used when speaking to her. Perhaps he remained guarded because they would be denied privacy.

'Will we be seeing Doctor and Mrs Hastings for breakfast this morning?'

The duke shook his head. 'Eve sent a message stating that they would be visiting patients in the area and would not arrive until supper, if then.'

'They are very dedicated to their work,' Maddie said, thinking that perhaps it might have been better that they not be so. Their devotion to medicine meant she would be alone with the duke.

'Indeed they are. That was quite a storm we had last evening,' he added. It was another benign comment.

'I hadn't noticed,' she lied.

'It has been some time since I've visited here,' he added. 'But I do not remember the weather being so volatile.'

If he was referring to her behaviour in bed, he could at least say so directly. She did not wish to be hinted at or handled. She had rather liked the man last night who had been both figuratively and literally naked with her.

But that man was gone and the Duke of St Aldric had returned, bringing all of his empty courtesy with him.

'That is probably because you spent so much time

in the nursery,' she snapped. 'I expect the view was quite different from there.'

It was wrong of her to strike in so vulnerable a spot. But it was very effective. At the mention of the nursery, his smile disappeared, replaced by something much more like a grimace. 'I did not take you to that wing so you could admire the view,' he said. 'I had hoped you would use your expertise as a former governess to suggest improvements to it. Now that you have had a few hours to think about it, what are your recommendations?'

So he wanted her expertise as a governess, did he? If that was all he wanted, then it was all he would have from her in the future. She looked him squarely in the eye, using the expression she saved for naughty children. 'You wish me to do what I can to make this place less grim for your heir? Then I will open the door to the hall, but nail the cabinet shut with your little toy people inside, until such a time as the child is old enough to understand the responsibilities he is to inherit. And then I will purchase some normal playthings.'

Apparently he had been hoping that she might suggest a cheery paint colour or a new rug. The bluntness of her actual recommendation wiped all expression from the duke's face.

Before he could speak, she continued, 'You asked for my help. I gave it. While you might understand the care and cutting of each blade of grass in your little kingdom, the land I am used to ruling is much smaller.

I know of children and the proper care of them. And I tell you that your perfectly preserved miniatures are not a toy so much as a source of terror.'

'They are necessary to teach the value of the holdings,' the duke said firmly.

'But keeping them spotless and unbroken for generations is unnatural,' she said. 'No one can go from birth to death without a little damage. It is nothing to fear. Children often learn from mistakes. If they are never allowed to make them, they have problems later in life.'

'I have made mistakes,' he said. 'You know I have, for you never tire of pointing them out.' He rose and threw his napkin onto the table. Then he departed the room with a slam of the door.

That was not what I meant.

For once, she had not intended to call him to task over Dover. Her concern was for the future, not the past, and the very real fear that their child might be tasked with the same impossible mission of maintaining his father's sainthood.

St Aldric was not infallible, any more than she. And after last night, she much preferred the real man to the facade. She might even be able to make a future with him, if she ever saw him again after this morning's argument.

When she had finished her breakfast, she'd almost worked up the nerve to go to him to try to explain. But by then he had sequestered himself in the study with Upton, the estate manager, and a line of tenants was forming in the front hall, readying themselves for a long-delayed audience with the duke.

At some point, she might have to face the crowd, as well. They would want to meet the duchess and to gawk at her as though she was the bear caged in the Tower of London. With this marriage, she had become a curiosity to be displayed for the masses.

But she could not manage it today. Not when she could still remember the rows of tiny people locked away in the nursery and worry that she might meet someone who had a passing resemblance to one of them. The thought gave her chills.

She turned away from the study and the front of the house to the French doors leading into the back gardens. If the London town house had been impressive, Aldric House was magnificent and the grounds around it were a reflection of that perfection. Walkways of crushed white stone and boxwood hedges separated the rose garden from the kitchen garden. Last night's rain was drying on the grass and the air was full of the smells of summer.

Best of all, it was natural, wholesome and real. The flower beds might be carefully tended, but they lacked the fearsome design of the bedrooms, or the aloof dignity of the ground-floor rooms. The plants here were well established and growing together like welcoming old friends. She wandered down the rows between them, which led her to the back of the house, and the stables.

She would not linger there for long. She had not grown any fonder of horses in the few days that had passed since her visit to Tattersall's. But as she passed one of the paddocks, she saw the animal a groom was leading towards the freshest green grass in the field.

'Buttercup?'

The horse did not answer to a name it had only heard once. But the sound of Maddie's voice made the big head swing in her direction, as though the nag was trying to remember why that particular sound seemed familiar.

'Aye, your Grace,' the groom said with a bow. 'That is what his Grace calls it.' The man said *it* as though he felt the word *horse* might not be appropriate. 'It is a sad thing, to be sure. But his Grace seemed to think that it was important to have it—who am I to question him?'

If she had saved it from the knackers, then it made sense to keep it with the other cattle. But that did not explain its presences in Aldricshire. 'I know this horse was in London just a few days ago,' Maddie said. 'Surely she did not walk all the way here.' At the time of purchase, she would have doubted that the beast could manage the trip from the auction to St Aldric's London stables. Yet here she was, forty miles away and as close to healthy as she was likely to be.

'No, your Grace. His Grace thought that the country air would be better for her old lungs, but she was not strong enough to make the trip on her own. She rode here in a wagon.' The groom smiled. 'It was

quite a sight when they arrived. I think it was an af-
front to the dignity of the St Aldric cattle to have to
carry one of their own. But Buttercup took it placid
as a milk cow.'

'He brought her here,' Maddie said again, still
amazed.

'And gave special instructions for her care,' the
groom added. 'He has already been down to visit her
this morning with a sugar lump and a carrot for her
breakfast.' The groom grinned. 'I cannot tell why
he has her. But he seems to think she is worthy of a
peaceful retirement. And she is grateful for it, pricks
up her ears when she hears his voice and comes like
a faithful dog.'

When she had purchased the poor animal, Maddie had not thought further than causing a moment's
aggravation. But a thing as large as a horse did not
simply evaporate once the joke was over. Now she felt
proper guilt for her actions. She had thought Buttercup good for nothing more than dog meat and glue
and had paid an exorbitant sum, not caring what was
to become of her other than that she might be a vehicle for revenge.

But St Aldric could not be moved to anger over a
thing such as this. Instead, he had rescued the horse,
just as he had spent his youth repainting model farms
and tending cotton-wool sheep.

Maddie held a cautious hand to the mare, who re-
garded her sceptically.

'Oh, come on, then,' she said in a matter-of-fact

tone. 'The duke may have cared for you, but I was the one who bought you in the first place. I deserve some small credit for it, don't I?'

The horse gave her an experimental nuzzle and then pulled away when she noticed the absence of treats.

She plucked a handful of clover out of the grass at her feet and offered it to the horse, who took it gingerly. 'See? There is nothing to fear here.' And it was true, was it not? There had been no danger to her, even if she provoked him. There had been no threat at all since the moment she had accosted the duke in the street. Last night they had lain together, but she had been the aggressor.

Three weeks ago, she could not have imagined it possible.

Maddie patted the horse's nose. 'It is a strange old world, Buttercup, full of unexpected events.'

The horse mocked her with an understanding stare and a deep snort that blew spittle onto her hand.

Maddie wiped her fingers on the grass and took the horse by the nose again, staring into its eyes with her best governess look. 'The next time I come to you, I shall bring a carrot. You had best accept it gratefully, or I shall have the grooms put a saddle on you.'

The horse looked properly chastened by the idea of a ride and snuffled her hair with grudging affection.

She took her leave of the stables in a more pensive mood than when she had come to them. Even if she had done the poor mare some good, she had been stupid and spiteful to buy it, thinking only of herself and her needs. It was wrong of her and she was sorry for it.

It made her feel rather foolish to have lectured the duke about the need to allow a mistake now and then. She had made a rather large one with Buttercup, but he had been the one to deal with the consequences of it.

The path she had taken from the house continued downhill towards the river. At the foot of the gardens there was a small, round building made of rough stone and spattered with bird droppings. She approached quietly, not wanting to disturb the residents.

She had never worked in a house with a dovecote. But now, it seemed, she was mistress of one. She enjoyed the taste of the bird, but today it would be soothing to see the soft grey feathers of doves and pigeons, to hear the cooing and perhaps to scatter some grain for them and watch them feed.

But when she poked her head into the room, it was not pigeons that looked back at her. The matched pairs of beady black eyes that looked down on her from the majority of the nesting holes were set in bright red plumage and the whistles and chirps were the same that she had heard on her wedding day.

The man tending them gave her a sad look. 'Welcome, your Grace. And thank you for honouring me with a visit.' He stared up into the rafters. 'Although I am not usually quite so upended as this.'

'You are having difficulties with the birds?' she

said, feeling the same twinge of guilt as she had at the stables.

'These new ones are putting the pigeons out of sorts. I suspect they'd pack off their nests and move to Rayland's property if they could manage it. But if they go, what am I to do with a bunch of parrots?'

'Lovebirds,' Maddie said softly. 'Abyssinian lovebirds.'

'Parrots are parrots,' the bird keeper said stubbornly. 'The brighter the bird, the more delicate their temper. Other than peacocks, of course. Those are just plain loud. But at least peafowl are big enough to roast.'

He was obviously unaccustomed to visitors, for he waxed to his subject. 'There is not much meat on these lovebirds at all. And if they be from Africa, then how will they winter? I shall have to set burners to keep them warm. But if I do not open a window, they will all die of the smoke. And they do live up to their names, it seems. I must gather the eggs each day, for they are paired up and cannot seem to leave each other alone. If I am not careful, we will be arse deep in parrots.' He snatched his hat off and bowed. 'Beggin' your pardon, your Grace.'

'You have my sympathy,' Maddie said, caught between amusement and horror at the thought of a waist-deep sea of birds. 'I will talk to his Grace about them. I am sure we can find homes for some of the pairs. They are all the rage in London.' She had been the cause of this problem, as well. But perhaps if she could get rid of the birds, she might be the solution.

But before she had even known there was a problem, St Aldric had dealt with it. Perhaps it was wrong to be thinking of the bible verse about knowing the fall of a single sparrow. But it seemed The Saint, much as he hated the nickname, had earned it by his behaviour. She thought again of the miniature sheep, the fishing nets of knotted string and the tiny farmers standing in front of each small house. There was no detail too small to be handled, no name forgotten, no hardship that could not be eased.

And then he had dishonoured a governess. How abhorrent that must have been to such a carefully ordered existence. She remembered his apologies and his insistence that this had never happened before or since. If it had not happened to her, she would have nothing but the rest of his life to judge him by.

And she would have given him absolution.

She thanked the bird keeper and turned back towards the house. As uncomfortable as it might be, she needed to talk with her husband and bury the past between them, once and for all.

Chapter Twelve

Children often learn from mistakes. If they are never allowed to make them, they often have problems later in life. Michael listened to the sound of his own steps on the mahogany floor of the hallway, as precise and modulated as ever. They were unvaried and he counted them without thinking. If someone had called upon him to recite the paces necessary to reach any room in the house, he'd have a number in his head before they could finish the question.

He had reached the door to his office. As an experiment, he broke step, letting his foot drag on the parquetry before continuing.

It felt wrong. His body struggled to be in step. As he crossed the threshold, it ought to be right, left, not left, right.

The only places he did not know by heart were the bedroom wings, where he had rarely been permitted. While his wife's part of the house might remain alien to him, he should at least take the time to learn his own domain. How else would he ever find comfort in it?

With a wife and child, he would be forced to spend time here. He could not raise a son in London and expect him to learn and understand his role as the next St Aldric. He'd had some half-formed thought that, when the time came, he would leave his wife here to deal with the house. But that had been when he'd thought to marry Evelyn. On their visit here, she had proclaimed the place quite charming. And he had made sure to show her only the main rooms, making up some lame excuse about the bedrooms not having been aired.

But he'd meant to dump her here and to let her sort out the details. Now, if he left, it would be Madeline and an impressionable child. He could not allow that until he could be sure that she would not use his absence to insert her own mad ideas in the place of his far more sensible ones.

He stopped. What knowledge of child-rearing did he have other than what his father had given him? As a boy, he had been miserably unhappy. And while he was mostly satisfied with his adulthood, behaviours that had seemed precise and orderly now seemed rigid. The care with which he'd kept the little animals in the nursery was not so much responsible as unnaturally fussy. They were but toys. He had not wished to make even the smallest error, knowing how costly it might be.

Once grown, he had refused to allow for the possibility that sickness or weakness might change the plans he'd set for himself. He had thought that his own body could be as easily controlled as a machine. When it failed him, he had been like a rudderless ship. And when he had strayed…

The fact that the root of his mistake needed to point out his flaws to him was all the more galling. When she was not hurrying to keep up with him, her gait was regular without being regimented. It was the step of a governess, a woman who brooked no nonsense, but was capable of changing course and altering plans when needed to keep ahead of her charges.

Last night, she had proven that she could be spontaneous, passionate and deliciously improper.

'Your Grace?' Upton was staring at him.

He had paused with one foot on either side of the threshold and was daydreaming about bedding his wife. He smiled at his estate manager and continued into the room, turning his mind to business.

After a brief meeting about the state of finances and projections for the seasonal profits, Upton went into the front hall and collected the first tenant in the line of those who had requested an audience with the duke. So many people to see him. Each one had a problem or a petition that would require careful thought and wise judgement.

He did not doubt his ability to deal with them fairly. It had simply become too easy to avoid these sessions by staying in London and allowing Upton to deal with the day-to-day running of the estate. But was it really fair to the people to do so?

The smiles on most of their faces assured him that it was not. Many came today to offer thanks rather than complaints, as though they were bringing tribute to an emperor. While he dared not admit it to the Regent, he expected it was similar to holding court and more than a little flattering.

He had missed his tenants, of course. But did he deserve this? He could feel the knowledge of the holdings that had been carefully drummed into him from birth slipping away from disuse. He glanced up at the man approaching the desk, searching for a name, and for a moment his mind was a total blank.

Then he saw the ham the man carried beneath his broad arm, which reminded him of pigs. But there was not a whiff of manure about this fellow, which meant butcher and not farmer.

'Old Joe?' He smiled at the man's start of recognition. 'Surely not, for it has been too long. Young Joe, then.'

'Not so young anymore, your Grace.' The man grinned back at him.

'But I see you have taken the shop in the village. Is your father still with us?'

The man nodded. 'And with enough teeth yet to test our wares and assure me that this was worthy of you.'

The ham. He remembered it well. Smoky, sweet, pink and cured, but not dry. Michael's mouth watered at the thought.

Joe noticed and produced a blade from his pocket, slicing expertly through the rind and offering a sliver of meat.

Michael took it and tasted with a sigh. 'Paradise. It is good to be home again.' And for a moment, the words were not a lie. There would be cheeses, ale and a loaf from Mrs Weaver. Strangely enough, Mrs Weaver was from a family of bakers, though the Bakers grew and spun flax. One by one, the names and faces were coming back to him with the flavour of the meat.

'Good to have you here, your Grace. And your bride.' Heads swivelled up and down the row, for many had brought gifts as an excuse to visit the manor, hoping to catch a glimpse of the new lady.

'I will relay your good wishes.' He tried not to let the thought of Madeline put a chill on his tone and passed the ham to his overseer for safekeeping, turning the conversation to thatching and glazing of cottage and shop, and the need to grade the road of the village before the rains of winter.

One by one, the people came and he greeted them, listened to their problems and accepted their gifts, asked about their children and their lives. While Upton took notes in his little leather journal, Michael filed the information carefully in that part of his mind reserved for important facts about the land.

The line was dwindling, but he sensed a change in the crowd, a murmuring at the back and an awed hush.

Madeline was lurking in the hall.

He cursed silently that her interest had turned to the house at such an inappropriate time. He'd given her no warning, no instructions on what might be expected of her, simply because he had not wanted another argument. Worse yet, there might be a veiled threat that she meant to embarrass him with more talk of his mistakes while he was surrounded by the tenants.

She had been improving of late. And after last night, he had hopes. Some things were obviously changing for the better. Their tryst had made him forget the nature of their marriage and the way she'd behaved in London. The temporary truce between them could end as quickly as it had begun.

But at breakfast, he had teased her until he'd managed to provoke an argument. Then he'd walked out on her and slammed the door. He had been foolish.

There was a growing murmur in the crowd beyond the office door as she moved through them. And the nearer she came to him, the more tense he felt. Perhaps appearances were deceiving. The only people they had seen recently were servants and Sam and Evelyn. Madeline thought too well of them to misbehave in front of them. She had been on her best behaviour and he had grown complacent. In any case, they knew him too well to give much credence to her bad opinion of him.

His people knew him, too, but not as well as they should. They were glad to have him back and they were full of hope that he might stay. Suppose she realised this and worked to widen the breach? She could set the whole region in an uproar with a few well-placed rumours. She would make him ashamed, both of his behaviour towards her and the woman he had chosen to be their duchess.

Embarrassing him in London was one thing. If she came between him and his people, he would grow to hate her. But it had not happened yet. He stood and smiled, ready to offer her the respect due to his duchess, whether or not she deserved it. Damn it to hell, he would greet her as a bridegroom if it killed him. 'Is that my wife I see, loitering at the back? Come here, my dear, and meet our tenants.'

She moved forward in a hesitant lockstep, her eyes wide. There was no sign she meant to make mischief. In fact, she looked intimidated, almost to the point of fear.

But frightened animals were often the most dangerous. He would be on his guard. He gestured her to his side and signalled Upton to bring a chair for her, but she wavered on her feet, unwilling to take it. Which meant that he could not sit either. Even a pleasant meeting day was tiring and he did not wish to stand through the last third of the petitioners.

The next family stepped forward. It was the Bakers, husband and wife and a girl of about fourteen, come to discuss the dry season and the possibility that the rent might be late. What did one have to weave when the flax had died? He nodded sympathetically while Madeline stood at his side in confused silence.

'But that does not mean we have nothing to offer,' Mr Baker said earnestly, despite his protestations that they need not worry. 'It is a trifle. A nothing, really. But our daughter is learning from her mother, as she should. And with the cloth we've made, she's hemmed a handkerchief. A wedding gift for your lady.' Cautiously, the girl held out the folded square of cloth, dropping her eyes and holding her breath as she waited for the reaction.

Michael's heart sank. If his wife wished to destroy the morning, she had been given the chance. She had but to take the thing and announce that it was nowhere near the quality on Bond Street. That while he might admire the St Aldric crest, he must see that the griffons were not quite equal, the monogram not quite centred. The cloth was not nearly fine enough for a lady's delicate skin. While it would be embarrassing for him, it would be crushing for the girl and humiliating for the Bakers, who had done nothing to deserve her enmity.

It was too late to order her away. One sly comment and the good feeling of the morning would be gone, the day ruined. It would be the sort of visit he'd feared and no amount of tumbling in the bed sheets would make him forgive her. He waited in silence for the inevitable.

'It is…' She reached for it. 'Is…' He could see her shoulders begin to shake, probably from derisive laughter. 'Oh, I am so sorry.' She crushed it to her face and stifled a wail. The linen was growing damp with her tears and the words seeping around the edges of it were barely coherent. 'So beautiful…touched… do not deserve…thank you…'

Mr Baker took a step back from the desk, obviously alarmed, but Mrs Baker shot a glance to her daughter and nudged the girl to a curtsey. 'You're welcome, your Grace. You honour us. We work in wool, as well. There is a fleece in our shop right now that could be made up into a wee blanket, soft as a cloud, just right for a babe's cheek.'

Madeline's watery eyes appeared over the top of the linen, soft and brown as a doe's despite the tears, and she gave the slightest nod.

Mrs Baker nudged her daughter again. The girl's mouth was as round as an egg as she dipped to curtsey a second time. Then the mother gave a triumphant smile at having happened on the best piece of gossip in the holding. She had not only given the first gift to the new duchess, she had found the real reason that his Grace had returned to the country after so long.

Maddie withdrew as soon as she was able to master her tears, and hurried to her room. But the garish decor made her feel worse and not better. Her cupboards were full of silk gowns and muslins in more colours than she could name. There was more here than she could need in a lifetime. And all of them were pulling tight across the bodice as her body expanded. They would not fit, even if she could find an excuse to wear them. Now they were hanging in this horrible bedroom, which was itself a mockery of extravagance. The dovecote was full of lovebirds. The pasture housed that pathetic nag that she had forced on St Aldric. None of it brought her any satisfaction.

She had thought St Aldric distant and insincere, but he had done everything he could to help her. The people who worked the land around them adored him. He knew them by name and watched over each and every one of them as though they were his own family.

Though they had never seen her before, they welcomed her with joy and with gifts, never suspecting that she came to them ready to do mischief at each turn.

She had been trying to make an enemy of her husband while telling herself that she had made a husband of an enemy. Soon she would bring an innocent baby into this horrible house and she had no idea how to go on.

The tears were coming again. This time she did not try to stop them. She felt small and alone. So she turned and fled the duchess's suite for a room where she could truly feel at home.

Some time later, the duke sauntered by the open door of the governess bedroom, as though trying to pretend that there was any excuse for his presence in the nursery wing other than searching for her. He hesitated on the doorstep, making no move to come closer to her. 'Forgive my asking, Madeline—but are you well? In the office just now, you were rather overset.'

She sobbed aloud again and held out a hand to him. Then she dropped it, not wanting to involve him in this pathetic display of emotion.

'Do you wish to return to your own room? I doubt this one has been aired.'

She shook her head.

'Do you wish me to summon your maid? Or Evelyn, perhaps?' He turned, ready to go.

'No!' She was not sure what she wanted, but it was not to be prodded with tea and company. The tears were coming faster now as the enormity of the changes in her life caught up with her. She was pregnant. And she had married a stranger. What had she been thinking? Had she seriously been planning to spend the rest of her life in anger? As a governess, she had been quite clear with the children she'd taught on the importance of living up to responsibility and not wasting time in petty squabbling. But who was to teach that to her?

And what to do with her new title, her new position and the obligations that came with it? And the fact that, last night, she had climbed into his bed and demanded to have her way with him?

'Oh, hell.' Apparently even a saint lost patience when confronted with illogical displays of emotion. But just as she was convinced that he was about to storm off and leave her to her tantrum, he came into the room and sat on the bed beside her. Then he put his arms around her and kissed her. His mouth sealed hers, trapping the escaping sob in her throat while his tongue stroked gently over hers.

For a moment, she was still unsure of what she wanted. Then she gave up and let him kiss her. It was nice, at least, until it became difficult to breathe through her stuffed nose. She pulled her mouth free, leaned into his body, put her face into his coat and wept.

She felt him stiffen. Did he despise her? She had been awful to him. And all along he had been trying to make amends. The thought made her weep all the harder.

A rational voice at the back of her head informed her that such thoughts were the madness of a pregnant woman. She'd had a logical reason to be angry. It did not make her horrible. But the same rational voice reminded her that it was her choice as well to decide that enough was enough, to forgive and to declare the matter closed.

She heard St Aldric sigh again. Exasperated, frustrated and ever so slightly affectionate. 'There, there.' His other hand came around her waist and he patted her on the back. 'It will be all right. Tell me what you need. Whatever it is. I will make it so.' And there was the sigh again, as though he was silently wondering if it was even possible to make her happy. 'What do you require of me? How can I help?'

It was so very *him* to say such a thing. He was thinking of her first, now that he'd found her in need. Had she ever seen him selfish in his desires? In Dover, of course. But last night, he had definitely been a generous lover.

'I saw the horse,' she whispered. 'And the birds.' She sobbed again. But this time she put her arms around his waist, clinging to him.

He sighed again, thoroughly confused, and hugged her in return, leaning back onto the bed, holding her to his side. He lay there awkwardly, his shoes upon the floor. She drew her legs up onto the mattress and curled against him, comforted.

He released her for a moment, fumbled in his coat to produce a handkerchief and offered it to her.

'Thank you,' she managed, 'but I have a handkerchief.' She held up the sodden lump that had been the carefully made gift.

He pressed his own linen into her hand and waited while she blew her nose in a most unladylike fashion.

'Better?' he asked. She could not see his face, but when she wiped her eyes and looked up, she saw he was smiling. It was not the tight, frustrated smile of vexation that she was used to. He was bemused.

'A little,' she admitted. 'I am sorry…to be so emotional,' she finished, still not sure that she wanted to apologise for anything at all.

'Sam assures me that such spells are common amongst increasing women,' he offered. 'You have nothing to fear from them.'

'Do you consult him in all matters pertaining to me?' she said, her tone drying along with her eyes.

'He is my brother,' St Aldric said, as though the explanation were a simple one. 'He assures me that his wife is more knowledgeable on the subject. But I go to him, since he has known of us from the first. He is also a physician.' There was a slight pause. 'And even if Evelyn is the authority, it would be deuced awkward to consult her on such a personal matter.'

'Because you were once betrothed?'

'Because she would torment me unrelentingly,' he said. 'And because she is female. For a gentleman to express curiosity about such things would be unnatural. Especially about such things as the previous evening.'

She gasped.

'Do not worry,' he said. 'I did not discuss the specifics. But I have ascertained that fluctuations in the humours, both pleasant and unpleasant, and an increase in certain appetites, strange cravings and preferences, can be blamed upon the fact that you are increasing. You will not be held responsible by me or anyone else.'

'Last night…' she said, not sure how to enter that into the conversation.

'Was an increase in appetite. I will not upbraid you with it. Nor will I mention it again,' he said, once again the most diplomatic of men.

'Then you did not like it?'

His head was resting again her hair and she could feel him laughing as his lips rubbed gently against the curls. 'Quite the contrary. It was incredible. But I will have no expectations that it will be repeated.

I mean to make no demands on you, just as I promised from the first.'

'I see.'

'However, should you wish to do it again, use me as you wish. I will humour you, because you are with child.' There was no artifice in the grin on his face.

The tears had stopped. And now she was laughing. 'How gracious of you.'

'As always, I am your humble servant.' But parts of her humble servant were pressed close to her and feeling somewhat less than humble. She squirmed against him, arranging herself so that she might be closer. It was wrong. It was the middle of the day and she was still in her walking dress. He had interrupted what he was doing to come and find her. For all she knew, half the village of Aldricshire was still in the receiving room, waiting for him to return.

'Madeline?' His voice was quiet enough, but she had never been so close to him that the sound of her own name vibrated against her skin.

'Hmm?' she said, putting an ear to his chest so that she might feel his next words as well as listen to them.

'I think, unless you want me to humour you immediately, that we should probably leave this bedchamber.'

'Because it has not been aired?' She made no move to let go of him. Instead, she rolled onto her side and adjusted her hips so that his growing erection was well placed between her legs.

'With each passing moment it becomes more difficult to go.'

'Harder, you mean?' She pressed her legs together, trying to trap him between her thighs.

'You are teasing me.' He did not seem annoyed by it. He was merely acknowledging the truth.

'And you are a very busy man,' she reminded him. 'You would have to be very quick about it, so as not to disrupt your schedule.' She cupped him from behind and squeezed.

He gave a single groan of frustration. Then his hand was on his breeches, tugging so hard she heard a button pop and the fabric tear. His mouth covered hers and his kisses were rough and hungry. His tongue filled her mouth as she bit and sucked in response. He was yanking up her skirt, leaving her uncovered, spreading her with a stroke of his fingers before sinking one of them deep inside her. 'Is this what you want, witch?'

It was delicious, this feeling glowing in her again as she clenched her muscles around it. But it was not enough. 'More,' she whispered. 'More.'

He withdrew his hand and entered her, hard and fast, his lips pressed to her ear. 'Minx.' He thrust hard as he whispered, 'Temptress.' He thrust again. 'You are driving me to madness.' And he was driving into her, relentless in his frustration, eager for satisfaction.

He was not the only one going mad. She was panting as she grabbed his cravat and yanked at the knot, opening his shirt so that she could ring his neck in kisses and then in bites. It was fast and wicked, and she could not seem to get enough of him. Her breasts were straining against the confinement of her stays. Her body was wet for him, and his size, the movement, his hands tearing at her hair, pulling her leg until her knee rested against his waist, so that he could go deeper, deeper....

She cried out as she broke, going limp against him, but he continued, his final thrusts stoking the fire in her to a low, hot glow. Then he stiffened and relaxed in her arms.

She drifted back to earth to face what had just happened.

His head lifted from where it had been nestling against her covered breasts. He was smiling. 'You look quite shocked, Madeline. Please do not tell me I misunderstood your intentions.'

Misunderstood the feeling of her hands on his bottom? What had made her do that, in broad daylight, when she'd been crying only moments before? 'No. You did not misunderstand. I am just surprised that I have such intentions. They come upon me rather suddenly, you see.'

'Then I am glad I did not miss them,' he said. He moved his hand from beneath her and rubbed idly at a muscle on his neck.

She looked at the spot he had touched. So he was not perfect, then. He had a blemish. A single scar, or rather a group of them. Three parallel lines running a few inches at the side of his throat. By day, his valet must use some skill to see that they were hidden by the cravat, lest they spoil the perfection that was St Aldric.

'What did you do there?' she said, curious at this single sign of vulnerability.

'This?' He smiled. 'I should think you would know the answer to that better than I.'

'I?' She leaned back, surprised.

He snatched her hand from his chest. The shock of it curled her fingers involuntarily into a claw. He dragged the tips of them lightly along the skin of his neck.

Each one marked the path of a scar.

'That night,' he said softly, 'when you realised what had happened, you scratched me. That was the moment I knew I'd made a mistake. When I awoke the next morning, the blood had dried on my shoulder. I should have taken better care. It is funny how quickly such a minor thing can go septic.'

'You were ill?' she said, surprised again.

'Hardly. A little redness. A week's bother, more or less. But they did not heal smoothly, as they should. Hence the scars.' The affected shoulder gave a small shrug. 'I did not deserve to leave that place without some mark of it. Now when I look in the mirror, knowing that the scars are there, just hidden by my linen, prevents further excesses.'

She had marked him. She felt an unnatural grief for having spoilt something so beautiful. 'I'm sorry,' she murmured.

He pressed her hand to his throat, covering it with his own. 'You have no reason to be. I am sorry for not being the man you wished for.'

But perhaps you are.

Wasn't this man what she had actually always wanted? Not because he was a duke, for she had never in her wildest dreams thought to want that. She had wanted someone to lie beside her, to share laughter, to make her feel safe and part of his life and family.

Someone to love.

His fingers covering hers were warm, gentle. Gentle man. That was what he was. They stayed just like that for several minutes, his body still rested in hers. But the place where their hands rested on his throat was a much more intimate joining. She could feel the pulse beneath her fingers. Each swallow. Each sigh. Slowly, she felt her own breathing, her own heartbeat, falling into synchronicity with his.

She had been so angry for so long. Not without reason, but it was so tiring to hold that anger. It had been like gripping an animal, always struggling to escape. If she loosed it, it might turn with fang and claw and devour her. But to hold it meant scratches, small, septic.

She closed her eyes and let it go.

Chapter Thirteen

It had been his first summer in Aldricshire in nearly five years. Although he still did not like the house, Michael had to admit that he had forgotten many of the pleasant advantages of spending the Season here. He smiled at the retreating back of the two last tenants, who, though they were not leaving as friends, had at least accepted his opinion on the boundary between their fields and would abide by it. Upton had set aside the heavy book of maps and was gathering up the ledger and the rent money.

The people here were happy. The land was prosperous and he enjoyed his long walks through it. His wife was healthy. There was a rosy glow about her that reminded him of the blooms in the garden: lush, sweet and intoxicating. If the servants thought it odd that he spent most nights with her in a small bedroom in the nursery wing, they said nothing to indicate the fact. Even the sanest man was allowed an eccentricity now and then. This would be his.

He could blame it on her, if he wished. It was simply the irregular mind of a pregnant woman and former governess nesting in a familiar place. She might even agree with him to save him embarrassment.

But it had been his idea. The mattress was better than the one in his room, possibly because of its more innocent past. The space was small and comfortable. There were no bad dreams in it. He slept each night like a babe, his arms wrapped around Madeline in the place where they had first made their peace.

Michael walked back to his study, shaking his head, still not sure what it was that had convinced her of his good intentions. Had it been something he'd said or done? If so, he'd have done it earlier. She had fallen to weeping and muttered something about horses and birds. Suddenly, the trouble had been over and she had been his.

She had always been desirable. He could not deny that he had admired her, even at the start. But he had concluded that his feelings towards her were no different from what he felt whenever he saw an attractive female. She was comely, therefore he wanted her. When she'd come to him that first time? A man would have to be a fool to refuse.

But in the past few months, she had grown into something more than a pretty girl. Her wavy brown hair had grown longer and the soft loops of it tickled his face when he kissed her. Her body was soft and full, like an extra pillow for his head as they slept together. Her huge brown eyes smiled more than they cried. But if she wept, she turned to him for comfort.

And when he had kissed her...

He felt the rush of emotion again. Affection, of course. But this was different. It was as though she was an extension of his own body. Perhaps it was the natural reaction that any man had when looking at the woman who carried his child.

Or was it love? Could it really be that easy to feel that emotion? He was still suspicious of it, for it had been a stranger to him until now. He had loved his mother, of course, but that had been quite different and seldom reciprocated. He had respected his father because he had been obligated to. Father had been St Aldric, therefore he deserved respect. But he had seen his parents so rarely that feelings of affection towards them were theoretical, not practical.

When he had first decided to marry, he had chosen Evelyn because he'd liked her. He had not loved her. He had not known her all that well if he'd thought that she could be moulded into a duchess. She was perfectly charming, and totally unchangeable. His brother was the only man who asserted any influence upon her at all, and he was welcome to her.

But being married to Madeline was different. He admired her quick mind. He did not dictate to her and she did not blindly obey. Yet they seemed to agree on many things, and managed well together. Each time she returned his kiss he felt something rush through him, as though he wanted nothing more in the world than to have the moment frozen in time for ever. Especially good were the nights they spent lying side by side on the small bed, talking softly of nothing in particular, whispering and joking until one or the other of them drifted off to sleep.

Was one supposed to be so happy and to have no reason for it? Compared to the quick and dispensable pleasures available to a single man, this joy seemed dangerous. What would become of him if it ended?

Here was his wife now, framed in the doorway, swaying slightly, and out of breath as though she had rushed to come here. It was not like her to be hurrying around the house in the middle of the day. He was on his feet and halfway to the door without a thought. 'Madeline?' Was something wrong?

She held up a hand, as though she could hear something he could not. She looked confused. 'I must talk to you,' she said, with a little gasp. 'In private.' She glanced at Upton in apology. 'If it is not too much trouble.'

'Of course not.' He gestured and the man exited with his ledger, shutting the door behind him. 'What is it? The baby?' It was far too soon for that. 'Is there something the matter? Should I summon Dr Hastings? Or Evelyn, perhaps?' He put a hand under her elbow, leading her forward into the room.

'No. No,' she said with a little laugh. 'There is nothing to be alarmed about. I do not need the doctor.'

'But if I can help you in some way…'

She smiled at him as though he had said something wonderful and took his hand, placing it on her abdomen.

There was a twitch. Then another. It was as though someone was running their hand against a curtain he was touching. And briefly, their hands had met.

Michael jumped in surprise and pulled away as quickly as if she'd had a wasp's nest hidden in her skirts. Then he placed it back where it had been and waited. It was happening again. The movement was slower this time, as though the other person had lost interest in the game and was settling back to nap.

It was the most miraculous thing he had ever felt. Life. Their child. He could see by the look on her face that she agreed. She was as excited for this as he was. Her face, her body, everything about her seemed to radiate happiness. And she was smiling at him.

'Well?' she said, for his hand was still on her belly and he had not said a word.

Though he was never at a loss for words, he was stunned to silence by the enormity of it. He had a wife—and he was going to have a child. In a place where he had never known anything but misery, he was happier than he'd ever been.

Because he was with her. And she was with child.

He shook his head and smiled.

She nudged him with her hand. 'Speak, St Aldric. Do you have nothing to say when presented with such an important piece of information? Your heir is healthy enough to be kicking me.'

Call me Michael.

It was the only thing he could think to say. But the fact that he had never heard her use his given name was not germane to the discussion. 'Amazing,' he said at last.

'It is, isn't it?' She smiled back at him. 'I should not be surprised by it. But still...'

'Nor should, I,' he agreed. 'But it is still amazing.' He kissed her quickly, because he could not resist the chance. Then he put both hands on her now-still belly, moving slowly over it, reaching up to touch her breasts.

'St Aldric,' she said breathlessly, taking his hands and moving them lower.

There was his title again, at a time when he had no desire to be so formal. 'Madeline?' he said in a response and pulled her towards the chair behind the desk.

'St Aldric,' she said a little more firmly. 'We are in a common room.'

'And no one would dare interrupt us,' he said.

'Do you not have work to do?' she reminded him. 'It is the middle of the day.'

'It can wait,' he said, kissing her throat. 'But I cannot. Let me touch you again.' He moved his hand lower so she could have no doubt as to what he meant.

'But in a chair?' She grabbed the arms and tried to stand. 'I am not quite so nimble as I once was, your Grace.'

'Still so formal with me, Madeline?' He dropped to his knees in front of her. 'Let us see what we can do to change that.' Then he pushed up her skirts and kissed her thigh.

Her breath caught and she murmured, 'It is broad daylight.'

'All the better to see you, my dear.' He kissed her again, running a finger under one of her garters to tease the flesh beneath.

'Suppose someone in the garden should pass by the window?'

'Then likely they will be very shocked to see this.' He pushed her legs apart and licked between them.

Her hands pushed against the arms of the chair, trying to rise, but it only brought her body closer to him. So he caught the lips of her and sucked them into his mouth and smoothed his hands down over her belly until she relaxed.

'Oh, my lord.' She released the wood and ran her fingers through his hair.

'That's better,' he whispered into her skin. 'Much better.' And yet still not quite right. He kissed her again, working moving his tongue slowly back and forth over her. Then he paused. 'Speak to me.'

'Darling.' She gave a convulsive shudder.

He kissed her again, harder, touching his tongue to her opening and dipping into it again and again.

'Oh, my sweet.' She was arching to meet him now, totally helpless to resist the pleasure.

'Totally yours,' he agreed, and went back to the little bud of pleasure.

'I love you,' she whispered.

The words caught him off guard. Was he expected to answer them? Instead, he responded with an unrelenting kiss that left her panting so hard it stopped all further speech. He tormented her for a moment longer until she was writhing in the chair. If she'd have said anything then, it would not have been proclamations of love. It would have been a plea for release. Then he sent her over the edge with a final flick of his tongue and laid his head against her thigh, waiting for her to calm.

When he looked up at her, she was breathless, silent and smiling.

He touched one of the dark curls in front of him and gave it a gentle tug.

'This was unexpected,' she admitted.

'We have done it before,' he reminded her.

'Not here.'

He nodded.

'But it was nice,' she admitted.

It had been more than nice. He had made sure of that. 'Thank you,' he said, matching her prim tone.

'You are not always so open to me in the middle of the day.'

But she was the one who would not call him by name. 'We have done this before,' he reminded her again.

She laughed then, in a way that he had not heard before. At least, not from her. It was the polite drawing room laugh he frequently heard in London, the sort that even Evelyn Hastings used on those rare times when she was trying to have manners. 'But even so, the Duke of St Aldric does not often go to his knees and pleasure me without a thought to what the household might say.' She straightened her skirts and stood, giving him a saucy wink. 'I am most grateful, your Grace. I will return the favour at a more decent hour, if you will meet me in the usual place at bedtime.'

'Your servant, madam,' he responded with the same false courtesy that she was using on him. They exchanged smiles and he blew her a kiss, and she was gone. The interlude had been enjoyable and he looked forward to the evening, for he was fortunate to have a most passionate and demonstrative wife.

But he could not shake the feeling that something had just gone very wrong.

Chapter Fourteen

Autumn was coming and life was good. But it bothered Maddie that she felt it necessary to remind herself of the fact so very often.

Judging by the kicks it had been giving her, in less than a month she would give birth to a healthy child. The fear that filled her when she thought of that was so different from what it had been, when this had begun. Then she'd wanted nothing more than to escape the inevitable. It would be a disaster for both her and the child she carried.

But now? She was still afraid, of course. What if the child was not healthy? What if she was not strong enough to bring it into the world? Or to mother it once it arrived? Suppose it was different from caring for the children of others? Suppose she did something wrong? With no one to teach her, how was she to manage?

It was silly to worry. Was she not a duchess? And would she not be one until the end of her life? Duchesses were not supposed to be afraid. She had wealth, status and at least one good friend, for Evelyn had become as close as a sister to her. She had even managed to get rid of all but two of the lovebirds. After the wedding, she'd received several pieces of polite correspondence from guests, enquiring about how to procure them. Each time, she had packed off a matched set, along with instructions for care.

The final pair she kept for herself, finding a gold wire cage and setting it in the corner of the duchess bedroom. Like it or not, the decoration suited them.

If she could manage that, she could manage one small child on her own. And she must remember that she was not alone. Despite what she had expected when she had agreed to the proposal, Maddie had found a husband who was totally devoted to her. He thought of nothing but her happiness and her comfort. Her life was safe, well ordered and happy during the day. At night she had a lover who played her body like a harp, knowing precisely what it took to arouse her, to bring her to climax and to calm her to sleep.

The only thing she did not have was his love. He cared for her as he did all of his other possessions, with total dedication. But there was a benevolent distance to him, as though he viewed her as a responsibility, albeit a pleasant one. St Aldric allotted her whatever portion of his heart was left, having already given the larger share of it to his lands and tenants. And beneath the title, there was still a thin layer of artifice that separated her from the true Michael Poole, on all but the rarest occasions. She suspected it would always be so. But it kept them from arguing about foolishness and prevented either of them from being hurt.

Eventually, she might learn to be satisfied with that. Devotion was nearly as good as love. She had learned from the loss of Richard that romantic love, while quite nice when you were in it, caused a great deal of pain when it left. She should be grateful, but it was difficult. The pain seeped around the edges occasionally, just as it had when she'd forgotten herself, announced her love for him and got no similar response.

She'd a mind to tell him that if he had not wanted her to fall in love with him, he could have done his part to prevent it. He could have been, in some small part, the man she had feared he was when she'd married him. He could have been the shallow, careless reprobate he had seemed on the night they'd met.

Instead, he had been lovable. In her weakened state, she had been happy to succumb.

But with practice, she was learning to be as he was, passionate at night, affectionate by day and unceasingly polite.

That was why she spent her mornings in the morning room and not lounging in the salon. She was prepared to receive company, even though she had no expectations of any. She visited the village, taking time to talk to the people there and learn their names and families. If she had married a saint, she must learn to be worthy of him.

The last thing she expected, when the butler finally came to announce that she had a guest, was that it would be someone from her own past. 'It is a Mr Colver, your Grace. He said you would know him.'

'Of course.' She rose, forgetting for a moment that she did not have to. After all this time, she had not expected a visit from the man who had taken her in as an infant. That he would seek her out now could not be good news. Joyous things came in letters and not surprise visits. She hoped he was not here to relay the loss of Mrs Colver. Though the pair of them had turned her out after they'd learned of her affair with Richard, she no longer felt bitterness towards them. It had worked out for the best.

Without thinking, she wiped her hands on her skirt to remove the nervous dampness from the palms and said, 'Bring him to me.' Then she sat again, trying to order her mind and use the tricks that she had learned from watching the duke. She put on the false but interested smile, rehearsed in her mind the correct questions about family and friends and the sympathetic speech she would give that might comfort the man on his probable loss, without displaying her own distress.

But the man who stood in the doorway was not the shopkeeper who had been a surrogate father for the first years of her life. It was the younger Mr Colver: the one person she had been sure was lost to her for ever.

'Richard!' She could not help the joyful exclamation or the way she ran into his arms. He was live and whole. There were no scars on his face and no limp when he walked. Despite all she feared, he had survived, right down to the curl in his black hair and the easy smile. This was the moment she'd waited for for so many years. Her love had returned to her just as she'd dreamed.

And it was too late.

He was trying to kiss her, just as he used to, with a smile on his face and a firm hand twined in her hair. But he could not hold her as he had because of the obstruction of her belly. And the shallowness of her breathing had more to do with the baby pressing against her ribs than it did a rising tide of desire.

It was her enthusiastic greeting that had led him on. Now she must put a stop to it. She worked to disentangle herself from his caress before he attempted to slip his tongue into her mouth and kiss her like a lover. He was acting as if nothing had changed between them, but if he had found her here, he must know it had. It was sad that she must be the one to break his heart, for she had never meant to. But their time was past.

'Richard,' she said again, taking a step away to establish some boundaries between them. 'I must apologise for the informality of my greeting, but you took me quite by surprise. And it is so good to know that you are well. Come. Sit. I will send for refreshment. I am sure we have much to talk about.'

The butler, who was normally polite and expressionless, was staring at the pair of them, shocked at the intimacy between her and this stranger. But he managed a stiff nod and said, 'Of course, your Grace.'

'Brandy, please,' Richard said to him with a smile. 'I am parched and we have much to talk about.'

Spirits in the morning. Maddie gave the butler a nod of permission and requested tea for herself, hoping that it would steady her nerves. Then she chose a chair by the window instead of the sofa she preferred, to be sure that there would be some space between them.

Of course, St Aldric would have managed mischief no matter where she sat. Just the thought of it made her hot.

Richard was beaming at her. 'You are looking well, my love. Is that blush on your cheek for me?'

'Women in my condition are prone to flushing,' she said hurriedly. She must not be annoyed with him for his bad timing, or his confusion about the change in her affections. Her marriage must have been nearly as great a shock to him as it had been to her.

'And I assume congratulations are in order?' he said with an ironic glance at her belly. 'I had not expected to find you thus when I finally returned. It has been nearly nine times nine months since last we saw each other.'

The footman was entering with the refreshment tray and she hissed at Richard to caution him. Until she could figure out what was to be done in such a situation, she had no wish to add to the gossip.

But Richard ignored her, blundering on as the footman retreated. 'When I left, I thought there was an expectation between us,' he said. He looked hurt. But after months with St Aldric, she was growing good at seeing behind false fronts. He might pretend to be upset about her perceived infidelity, but he was too pleased with the quality of his brandy to be convincing.

'I thought you dead,' she said flatly. 'The Horse Guard could tell me nothing of your whereabouts after the Battle of New Orleans. I spoke with your parents, and they knew nothing either.'

'Probably because I had not contacted them until just last month,' he said with a dismissive wave of his hand. 'You know my father had no patience for me when I refused to take over the shop from him. It was why I bought the commission.'

'He was upset because you took money from the till without asking,' she said as gently as possible. Richard had been stubborn then, as had his father. The fights had been horrible. 'And they did not approve of what happened between us. I was not welcome in the house after you left. But the school did not mind if I remained there during holidays.'

'Do you blame me for that now?' He looked indignant.

'Certainly not,' she said hurriedly. 'It did not matter so very much to me. But I did miss you, once you were gone. To hear not a word, even after the war had ended…' There was probably a logical explanation. Soon he would tell her of a wound followed by fever and a recovery in some distant sick ward. He would assure her that contact had been impossible. Then she could go back to feeling sorry for her betrayal instead of annoyed that he had waited so long to come to her.

He smiled in the same knowing way he had when he'd seen her. 'I was busy.' He glanced down again. 'Just as you were.'

Busy. She deserved more than that after all this time. Months had turned into years. Had he really been too busy to write to his true love? There was no point in resurrecting the exact reason for his disappearance. 'I am married now.' Any marriage, for any reason, meant a permanent parting from Richard.

'So I see.' Richard was still trying to look hurt.

'I waited,' she reminded him, lest he think her too changeable. 'I waited for years. And I did my best to make it easy for you to find me if you returned. I wrote your parents as well, with each change in position.'

'When I visited them, they gave me your last letter and informed me of your intent to move again,' Richard said with a smile. 'But when I went to find you, another governess worked in your place. And your employer told me a most interesting story. And then there was the announcement in *The Times* of the sudden marriage of the Duke of St Aldric.'

He knew. Perhaps not everything, but enough to guess what had happened.

'There was an embarrassing misunderstanding,'

she said, amazed that she was saying such a thing. 'For a time, it was all quite difficult. But we have settled things between us and are quite happy now.' Not as happy as she might have wished, but better than she had ever imagined.

'It is a comfort that you did so well from it and avoided any scandal.' There was a dangerous pause. 'Because of an accident in Dover, St Aldric made you a duchess.' He looked down again. 'I suppose that it is his child you carry?'

'Suppose?' This hurt even worse than his expression. 'Of course it is his. Who else's could it be?'

Richard shrugged. 'There was a rumour about that he was unable. And you must understand, after what we were to each other, that I of all people know that you are quite willing...'

'I loved you!' Surely he did not think her some common trollop.

She heard an approaching footstep in the hall, louder than usual, as though someone wished to be heard before he entered. A moment later, St Aldric stood in the doorway, smiling and gracious, pretending that he had heard nothing of the previous conversation. 'I was told you had company, my dear. A Mr Colver?' He was looking at Richard, as though weighing him with a glance. 'Am I to meet a member of your family at last?'

Maddie rose to encourage Richard to get to his feet. 'Your Grace, may I present Mr Richard Colver.' She would not stammer or flush. She was the Duchess of

St Aldric and should be more than able to handle such a temporary awkwardness as introducing her former lover to her husband. 'He is the eldest son of the family who raised me.'

Richard had the sense to bow, and St Aldric acknowledged him with a nod of his head and a smile that was several degrees cooler than normal. 'Mr Colver.' Michael put a slight emphasis on *Mr.* It was unusual, for he never felt the need to point out another's inferiority.

Perhaps there was some military rank she could use when addressing Richard to make a better impression. She chided herself for this sudden snobbery. Had a few months with the duke really changed her so much? At one time, she'd sworn that she did not need money or rank to wed Richard Colver. But neither did she enjoy her husband's insolent pleasure at the lack of them.

'Maddie and I are old friends, your Grace. Very old, very dear friends.' Why could not Richard manage to behave as a gentleman? He was a shopkeeper's son in the house of a peer. Their old friendship did not give him right to such a possessive smile and the deliberate use of a diminutive that St Aldric did not make use of himself.

'Of course,' the duke replied. 'She speaks of you often.'

'Does she really?' Richard was grinning in response, as though wondering about the truth of this. But he could not be as surprised as Maddie was. At times, St Aldric might be evasive. But she had never heard him speak total untruth.

'But I have not seen Richard in a very long time,' she reminded them both. 'Years, in fact.' She looked at Richard again. 'As I told you, I thought you dead. In the Battle of New Orleans.'

Richard responded with a puppet-like nod, as though he were only agreeing with a complete falsehood to keep the peace.

'He saw the announcement of our wedding and sought me out to offer congratulations,' she finished, for her husband's sake. It might not have been his reason for the visit, but it was the only one she was willing to accept. 'Now that you have done so, Mr Colver, you must be eager to continue on to visit your parents. They are in Norfolk,' she added, to assure St Aldric that this would not be a regular occurrence. 'That is quite a distance from here.'

'Then I expect you will want to rest before your travels,' the duke said with his usual false smile. 'If it has been years since you've talked, there is much you must wish to say, if you are indeed such old and dear friends.'

'I am sure that Mr Colver has other plans,' she said hurriedly.

'On the contrary, I am at liberty.' Richard smiled back at the duke, ignoring her attempts to put him off.

'Then you must stay with us as long as you like,'

the duke said, the picture of hospitality. 'In fact, I insist upon it. Should we put him in the red suite in the west wing? The view is lovely. It will be most convenient, I am sure.' The phrase was innocent enough, but she knew his meaning. The red suite was part of the discreet maze that connected to her bedchambers. He was asking if she meant to cuckold him. To carry on as his mother had, entertaining lovers while he was still in the house.

'That will not be necessary,' she said, firmly hoping that it would reassure him.

'That will be delightful.' Richard had talked over her objection, accepting before she could find a way to put him off.

'The blue rooms are much more suitable,' she insisted. 'They are larger and more convenient to the servants.' And less embarrassing, since they were nearer the head of the stairs and opened onto the main corridor of the wing. 'I will speak to the housekeeper immediately and arrange for them to be opened. If you gentlemen will excuse me?'

It was a risk, leaving the two of them together to compare stories. But she had other things to worry about. The staff must prepare a guest room in a house that was not fit for guests. And she must invite… No. She must demand the company of Sam and Evelyn at dinner. A few minutes alone with the two men had seemed an eternity. She did not think she could stand to take supper alone with them, as well.

But first and foremost she must find Peg and tell her to lock all doors in the duchess wing that were not the blue suite, especially any that connected to her own room.

Chapter Fifteen

So this was the man that his wife truly loved.

Michael could not help but be disappointed, for he'd thought that she had better taste. He supposed Richard Colver was handsome enough, with thick, dark hair and the devil in his eyes. If she'd known him all her life, Madeline might have been too young and naive to resist his charms when he'd first seduced her. But it did not explain what the man was doing in his house and why he had heard his wife protesting that she loved him.

Now that Madeline was gone and they were alone together, the lout had the gall to stare back at him with a smug smile upon his face, all but announcing his previous intimacy with Michael's wife.

The duke waited. And waited still longer, until nearly a minute had ticked by and the smile of the man at last began to fade. Then he walked to the sofa and arranged himself upon it, gesturing to the most uncomfortable chair in the room. 'Please, Mr Colver. Let us sit.'

The interloper took the offered chair and tried to find a comfortable position in it, then reached for his brandy.

Michael stared at the glass, making no comment about it one way or the other. But the intense gaze was a reminder of the fact that the man who paid for the liquor had the sense not to drink it before noon.

Colver set it aside again.

'So, Mr Colver—' he smiled '—I am always interested in meeting friends of my wife. Please, tell me about yourself.'

Colver's silence to this was telling. In Michael's experience, men who paused significantly when asked such a simple question were searching for the best lie to tell. 'I am an old friend of Maddie's.'

'So you said.'

'And a veteran of the war in the Americas,' Colver added.

'The Battle of New Orleans,' Michael reminded him. 'But that was several years ago, was it not? What has occupied you since?'

'That is of little importance,' Colver said.

Which likely meant drinking and gambling and whoring.

'When I discovered that Maddie had married, I was eager to renew our acquaintance and assure myself that she was happy.'

'She is.' He was unaccustomed to making such

blanket statements for her. But who better to do it than the man who shared her bed each night?

'We were quite close, your Grace.' Colver was smiling again, regaining his confidence. 'One might even say we were betrothed.'

'Either you were or you weren't,' Michael said bluntly. 'Which was it?'

And there was the pause again. 'We had an understanding,' Colver said. 'She agreed to wait for me while I made my fortune so that we could be married.'

'How unfortunate that you did not arrive sooner.'

'Unfortunate indeed, your Grace. I would have withdrawn from the situation had she not reached out to me, speaking of her unhappiness and her longing that we might be together again.'

It was obviously an untruth. She would never have said such a thing. At least not lately. He was sure of it.

'And when she told me of the unfortunate circumstances of your meeting, the uproar in the night when you were discovered....'

He knew about Dover. Who could have told him of that but Madeline? Had his wife's sudden change in manner towards him been nothing but a trick? Of late she had seemed aloof. And there was the continual use of his title.... What did he really know of women?

Most important, how well did he know Madeline?

Nothing would be served by ejecting the man from the house before he understood the extent of the problem. 'Whatever occurred has been settled between us for some time. She is married and with child.'

'I had not expected that she would marry another,' Colver argued. 'But the fact that she is with child is not so big a surprise. When one is in love, one is sometimes less than careful about such things.'

'She deserves none of the blame for this,' Michael said, conscious of his wife's honour. 'I was the one who was careless that night.' And she had not loved him when they had conceived.

'But we were very much in love,' Richard admitted.

Suddenly, Michael realised that they were talking at cross-purposes. He had been blurting awkward statements to a man whose meaning had been quite different.

He felt like a fool.

He had been sure of only one thing in the past nine months. Despite his fears, he had been able to father a child. But suppose Colver spoke the truth and Madeline had rushed to him with another man's baby?

No matter what had passed between them, this man had waited until he was sure Madeline had married well before coming to her aid. His behaviour was suspect and his answers to other questions had been evasive. There was no reason to believe him now.

But there was always the possibility that, in this, he spoke the truth. Michael's doubt was small. But if he was not careful, it could grow like a worm in an apple.

'So you were in love,' Michael said, dismissing something that had no part in the discussion. 'How fortunate for you. But I fail to see what your lost love has to do with my wife and my child.' No matter what the truth might be, and what he might feel for a woman who could not even call him by name, he was positive he hated Richard Colver.

'We will not argue about the parentage of the child, for that is beneath contempt.' But Colver smiled as he said it as though he had no doubt of the truth, but wished to humour his host. 'Maddie is another matter entirely. She claims she thought me dead. Accepting your offer was clearly an act of desperation.'

Then take her and be gone. It was the wounded cry of his heart. But since Michael was not even sure he had a heart, he ignored it. 'You assume, now that you have finally arrived, that she would prefer to go with you.'

'We would leave the baby with you, of course,' Colver said.

'How magnanimous of you,' Michael responded.

'But should that child be a girl, it would be quite awkward, would it not? Then you would have no heir and no wife.'

Or he could succumb to instinct and have Colver thrown into the street. Then he would lock the doors of the duchess wing with his wife inside and visit her nightly until they had a son. There would be no further nonsense about escaping from a life of luxury with an itinerant soldier.

Then he imagined Madeline tugging helplessly on an immovable door, just as he had done so long ago. Madeline, to whom he had promised everything, including her freedom, should she want it.

'Of course, we might handle this in another way,' Colver suggested to fill the silence. 'A simple settlement for the loss of her affections and I will take my broken heart and go.'

'You wish me to pay you to leave her?' Michael laughed. 'It did not take money to make you go away before.'

'But now I am concerned with her welfare. After what happened in Dover...' He shook his head in disgust. 'I could not part from her so easily,' he said.

'You wish me to buy you off.' Michael thought about this for a moment and laughed again.

'We were practically married,' Colver repeated.

Then Michael rose and advanced on the man. Colver was the taller by a tiny margin. One hoped a trained soldier would have skills to defend himself.

Colver raised his hands, ready to fight.

'Before you strike, remember who it is you hit. It is more than a simple crime to slap a peer. You will hang for it.' It was a pity, really, for Michael most wanted to punch the man. But it would not have been fair to provoke a fight just to see his opponent arrested.

'Then do not threaten me,' Colver said with a stammer.

'I am not threatening,' Michael said with a smile. 'It is more of a promise. If you go from here, it will not be because I paid you to do it. I might have the power to buy you off, but if I do, you will be back again when the money runs out. I have the power to make you disappear. A word from me and you will be in Newgate. Two words and you will hang.'

'You would not dare,' Colver said with no real conviction.

'I would not bother,' Michael said in response, 'unless Madeline requests it of me. My affection for her has kept me from interfering so far. Since you are such an old friend of hers, I would not deny her your company. If, once our child is born, she wishes to go with you, I will not stop her. I promised her anything. And I mean to give it to her, even if what she wishes is you.'

Michael stared at the man until he was sure that Colver understood what an unworthy choice he was, and then continued.

'But if Madeline grows tired of you, or you annoy her in any way, God help you. There is no telling what might happen. What with the pregnancy, she is in a most volatile frame of mind. I suggest, whatever she might decide to do with you, that you treat her well. For if you hurt her, I will end you.'

And then he excused himself from the room to give his wife's lover the privacy to run or stand his ground.

For the first time since he'd come back to Aldric House, Michael locked the door behind him before taking to his own wing. He did not like locked doors, even when he held the key to them. Tonight, however, the less he knew about what went on in the rest of the house, the better.

He had hoped that the problem might have solved itself after his terse conversation with Colver. But though the man was not particularly smart, he was persistent. He had moved into the room that Madeline had selected for him and would likely be there until someone put him out by force. Since Michael had no intention of intervening, it would be up to his wife to settle the matter.

Dinner had been a tense affair, even with Madeline's attempt to keep things civil by inviting the Hastingses. Colver had taken any chance to remark on his close association with Madeline, trying to turn the conversation to mutual friends and jokes that only they would understand. Madeline was clearly uncomfortable, looking the way he had felt in their early days together, when he expected any word from her mouth to be a snide reminder of the past.

But the tone had changed when Sam had found his own reason to dislike the newcomer. After the ladies retired to the parlour, Colver had mentioned his service in the army. The former navy doctor had turned the conversation to detailed analyses of every battle fought in the past fifteen years, while making sure that Colver's glass was never empty.

When the precious Richard had staggered from the room to relieve himself, Sam had announced, 'If that man is an officer and a gentleman, then I am Lord Nelson.' He went on to say that, while the man appeared to have served in the campaign he described, his knowledge of the battle was probably gained by watching it over his shoulder as he deserted his comrades.

Colver had returned to the room, Sam had opened another bottle and things had gone downhill from there. By the time Evelyn had collected her remarkably clear-headed husband for the walk back to the dower house, the servants had been forced to carry an unconscious Colver to his room. Michael was already feeling the effects of too much port and the folly of trying to keep pace while drinking with the military.

Now there was a knocking on the locked door, assuming the hammering was not just in his head. He glared at Brooks, the valet. 'See to that. And tell whoever it is that I am not in the mood for company.' Then he kicked off his own boots and stretched out upon the bed, waiting for death or morning.

But the valet did not return. When he opened his eyes a few moments later, Madeline was standing before him, hands on hips.

'Do not look at me in that way,' he said, too tired to pretend that he was not angry.

'And do not hide behind locks when I wish to speak to you. I told Brooks if he tried to prevent my entry, I would call the footman and have the door removed from its hinges.'

'Very well,' he said. He folded his hands behind his head and leaned back against the headboard, trying to maintain his calm. But for once he did not wish to settle things diplomatically. He wanted an argument. 'What do you wish of me?'

'I want to know what you intend to do about our guest.'

'Colver is your problem, not mine.'

'But you did not need to invite him to stay,' she said. 'Nor did I appreciate your attempt to place him next to my bedchamber.'

'Was that not what you wished?' he said. 'When I came upon you this morning, you were declaring your love for him.' It was a word, nothing more. And though he was uncomfortable when she said it to him, he hated to hear it applied to another.

'I did love him,' she said, refusing to deny it. 'But that was in the past. Did you expect me to lie about it, as you did when you said I told you of him?'

He laughed. 'What a curious omission that turned out to be, for I am sure it is an interesting story. I was not lying. You did not mean to tell me of him. But I learned of him all the same. You were weeping for him in your sleep on the night we married. Begging him to rescue you. From me.'

She looked shocked at this and he could not resist adding, 'You still call his name in your sleep sometimes when we are together.'

'We were to be married,' she snapped, as though that was explanation enough.

'And you believed that?' He laughed again, enjoying her discomfort. 'He never meant to marry you, you stupid girl. He tricked you out of your maidenhead. Then he left you. I wonder how many other fiancées he ran to the army to escape. And how many he has gained since returning.'

'That cannot be true.' Her voice was soft and trembling with rage.

'Did you imagine him remaining celibate for you, all the long years?' Perhaps tomorrow he would regret how much pleasure it gave him to hurt her with the reality of it, but tonight it was vindicating. He raised his arms to heaven and then dropped them. 'But I forget. You claimed you thought him dead. He looks whole enough now, does he not? I am sure, when next he tricks you out of your clothes, you will find his body unmarked.'

'How dare you?' She was white with rage, swaying on her feet, as though the burden of carrying both the truth and the baby was too much for her.

'How do I dare?' He touched his own breast with a forefinger. 'I am sorry if you do not wish to acknowledge the obvious. But what a surprise that now that you have married me, he's located his lost love. What could be so different?' He laid the finger on his chin, as though contemplating. 'I would guess he is after two things—to bed you and to be paid to go away after.'

When she spoke, her voice was as dead as her complexion. 'If you are so sure of this, then I ask again, why did you invite him to stay?'

She was standing so close to the bed that he could smell her perfume while she stared at him with those bottomless dark eyes. Something at the core of him was shouting that he should stop being an ass and admit his mistake. Then he could order the lout from the house and things could return to normal.

Instead, he spoke the truth.

'Because I could not resist the chance to acquaint myself with your tragic lost love. And to discover if it is true that, as you insist, you have not seen him in years.'

'Why should it not be true?' The fact that she could not guess his intent was proof of her innocence.

But he could not stop badgering her. 'Do you deny that you were intimate with this man?'

By the look on her face, he knew that he had uncovered the one secret she had wished to keep. 'On the night we met, I never claimed to be innocent. I didn't get the opportunity to.' Her voice was still quiet, but in shame, not anger.

'You let me assume it ever since,' he reminded her.

'Because you wished it to be true,' she said, shaking her head. 'But did you ever question, your Grace, how there come to be so many fallen women in this country for you to make sport with? Not everyone can afford to be as pure as you expect them to be. Nor are some of us so fortunate as to have married the first man we loved.'

'Fortunate?' he said with a smile. 'You think it would be fortunate to have married a deserting soldier instead of a duke?' Perhaps she did. If she loved Colver, she would have wanted to marry him.

She had claimed to love Michael, as well. It was another proof that words were cheap.

'On the night we met,' she said, 'I had chosen to meet my new employer in Dover for a reason. That was the inn where I had stayed with Richard the night we said goodbye. I prayed that he would come for me and give me children of my own. It was him I was hoping to see. You came to me instead.'

'So you say.' It explained the welcoming arms he remembered and the way she'd cried in her sleep. But there was another possibility. 'It does not explain how I came to be in the wrong room that night,' he said.

'You were drunk,' she reminded him.

'I had never been so drunk before that I could not find my way.'

'There is, as they say, a first time for everything.'

'Or you could have learned of my identity and tricked me into the wrong room. It would have been a most profitable way to explain an indiscretion that had already taken place.' It was a wild assertion, but it made as much sense as what had actually happened between them.

She gasped. 'You think that I was already with child?'

'It would have been extremely convenient for you to find a member of the peerage drunk enough to be gulled into taking on this mess.'

'How dare you?' He had forgotten the voice she had used upon him in those first days when she had hated him. 'It is one thing to doubt me. But to doubt your own child? That is beneath despicable, St Aldric. The baby is yours. Do not think to deny it now.'

'That is just it. I can't deny it. I have accepted you for all to see as my wife and the mother to my heir.' It was happening again, just as it had in Dover. He had drunk too much and gone too far. But this time he was hurting her with words, displaying every irrational fear without thinking of the consequences.

'Then let me assure you,' she said, stepping back out of reach of him. 'You may believe what you like. But I am willing to swear on the Bible, if there is one to be found in this den of iniquity, that the child I carry is yours. I had not seen Richard for years before this morning. When I parted with him, it was in the sincere belief that he would return for me and make me his bride.'

'Very well,' he said, wishing that a simple agreement could take back the horrible things he had already said.

'But what I do not understand is why it should matter to you who I love, or who I am with?'

'You are my wife,' he reminded her.

'And you promised me, from the first, that you wanted nothing more from me than the child.'

Of course he had. But had she forgotten what had happened these past months? 'I thought…'

'That there might be something more between us?' She smiled sadly. 'So did I. I even embarrassed myself by announcing my love for you. Since you did not answer in kind, I have come to assume that my feelings are not reciprocated. If that is true, you can hardly demand that I be faithful to you.'

'You are my wife,' he repeated.

'And you, St Aldric, are blind to your surroundings.' She glanced at the room around her. 'Your parents were married, were they not? Did they not teach you what it means to have a marriage in law and not spirit? You want someone to share your bed. I understand that, for it was what I wanted when I came to you that first time. And when we are in bed we suit well together. But I will not always be young and pretty. Some day you will tire of me, and that will be the end of it. You will take a lover and I will regret that I did not leave when you gave me the chance. Now, if you will excuse me, it has been a trying day. And, much as I might like to, I lack the energy to leave you tonight.'

Chapter Sixteen

To Maddie, the arrival of Richard Colver was proof that one did not necessarily want to have one's prayers answered. She had waited for this moment for so long, never thinking that it would be unwelcome or that Richard would turn out to be anything less than the handsome hero she remembered.

Last night at dinner, his easy smile had looked more like a leer. She could see traces of grey in his hair, the red in his eyes and the sallowness of his skin. The changes looked more like dissipation than age. And during what should have been a polite dinner, she had caught him admiring both her bosom and Evelyn's as though he expected them to be served for pudding. He had no trouble availing himself of his Grace's meat and wine, shovelling the food into himself as though he could not decide whether to eat or stuff his pockets and run.

Had he always been like this? Because it seemed that the duke had been right: the man to whom she'd given her innocence was a selfish, greedy swine. He had not loved her then any more than he did now. She could not imagine he was here for any reason but to make trouble.

And he had succeeded. It had led to the row she'd had with St Aldric before bed. If he had simply been jealous, she might have flattered herself that he cared for her more than he did. Judging by the smell in the room, he was as drunk as he'd been on the night in Dover. Though he might promise that the scratches on his shoulder were enough to keep him sober, they had failed to do any good yesterday. He'd questioned her honour and accused her of lying about something so important as to the paternity of their baby. His doubts hurt far worse than the absence of loving words.

It had been a miserable few minutes, but she had come away with a new understanding of several things. For one, she was sure that she wanted nothing to do with Richard Colver. She would not go so far as to call herself a fool for loving him. She had been an innocent, young girl and could not have known better, but only an idiot would go to him now.

Another less pleasant truth had come out, as well. She still loved St Aldric, even after the horrible things he had said. But he had made no similar declaration, nor did she suspect one was on the way. When confronted with difficult truths, he'd announced she was his wife, treating her like any other property. He had not cared enough to keep her safe from Richard. In fact, he'd gone out of the way to throw them together.

She would have no help from her husband in ridding herself of this nuisance, since he did not care enough about her to remove the man himself.

She doubted Michael would welcome her infidelity. In fact, he seemed to expect it, even though she'd given him no reason. Nor had he promised her that he would be faithful. When she had told him he'd grow tired of her, there was no vehement rejection of it. When given a chance to prove her wrong, he had not promised to cherish her for ever. He had simply stared at her, as though amazed that she had the nerve to point out his hypocrisy. It showed that he felt nothing at all for her other than hurt pride that she had not been a virgin when he had first lain with her.

If they were not careful, they were destined to follow the path of his parents. And, much as he claimed to hate the past, he was doing nothing to prevent the repetition of it.

She would leave before that happened. She did not want to see women sneaking into the duke's chambers, nor did she wish to flaunt lovers in front of him. In the past months, she had begun to imagine a future for them that was quite different from the original plan. They would share a life together. There would be a houseful of children. Even if St Aldric could not manage to love her, he would adore the children. Wasn't that what he'd wanted all along?

If not, she would have enough love for all. She absently touched her stomach, as though she could offer some reassurance to the baby resting so close to her heart.

But now she was back to the place she had started: in a loveless marriage and about to produce a single child.

This morning, when she came down to breakfast, there was no sign of St Aldric. Richard was sitting at the head of the table as though he belonged there, with heaped plate and an ironic smile.

Maddie made a mental note to invite Evelyn and Sam to every meal from now on, even if it was necessary to claim illness to get them to the house. 'Good morning, Mr Colver.'

'Good morning, your Grace.' He stood for a moment and bowed, then sat and went back to eating.

She enquired after the duke. The footman informed her, with a meaningful cough, that his Grace had elected to take meals in his room. She'd have called him a coward for refusing to meet a rival, but to force himself to stay in the duke's wing, a place he could hardly abide, was its own sort of punishment. After last night's excesses, she hoped his head ached, as well.

For herself, her appetite had fled with the argument and no amount of Wow-Wow sauce was likely to bring it back. She had slept poorly as well, for the baby would not allow her a moment's comfort.

But neither St Aldric's suffering nor her own rid her of the problem at hand. 'Well, Mr Colver,' she said again, unsure of how to start the conversation. 'it has been lovely seeing you again after all this time.'

He grinned at her, taking another swallow of coffee. 'And more than lovely to see you, my dear. It is good to find that you have fallen on your feet after the time we spent together.'

As opposed to falling on her back? she wondered. Many women in her situation had been forced into a far more dishonourable course of action after being abandoned by a lover. 'Now that you have assured yourself of my safety, you will most likely want to be moving on,' she suggested.

'I see no reason why I should. Your husband invited me to stay as long as I wished,' he reminded her.

'But that does not explain why you are here in the first place,' she said.

'I wanted to be sure that you are happy,' he said.

If he had two good hands but had not written her, then her happiness had not occurred to him in several years. 'Your concern for me is touching,' she said, 'but unwarranted. Now that I am married, I am quite secure.'

He sighed. 'It is a shame that we are not all so fortunate.'

He referred to himself, she supposed. But she was at a loss as to what he expected from her. She thought for a moment and put on an attitude of optimism and encouragement, just as she did when dealing with sulky children. 'It is true that life can be difficult. But when one perseveres and applies oneself to betterment, there is no telling what can be accomplished.'

'A noble sentiment,' he agreed. 'Success is possible when circumstances do not work against one. When one is betrayed by a lost love, for instance. With marriage comes certain expectations, and the dissolution of a betrothal ends them.'

True, she supposed, but how did it pertain to this situation? 'Since I have married,' she assured him, 'no damage was done.'

'To you, perhaps.'

It took her a moment to realise that he was referring to himself, but his dejected look was spoiled by the fact that his cheeks were bulging with St Aldric's bacon. 'You cannot seriously claim breach of promise,' she said.

'You promised yourself to me. Then you abandoned me to marry St Aldric.' He had the nerve to look injured.

'Because I thought you were dead,' she reminded him, snorting in disgust. 'Next you will be saying that I took your honour.' St Aldric was right. The man was an ass. He had used her and abandoned her. Now he was trying to find a way to use her again.

'I would not have made love to you had I not thought you serious and constant in your affections,' he said. 'In waiting for you, I have denied myself the opportunity to marry well. Now I have nothing. Not even you.'

The fact that she placed last in value told her everything she needed to know about his true feelings for her. 'And what do you expect me to do about your tragic circumstances?'

'Normally a settlement is in order.'

She smiled, for to this she could answer. 'Then you are talking to the wrong person, Richard. I have nothing to give you.'

'But you are a duchess,' he said, confused.

'With not a penny in my pocket,' she said, confident that it was the truth. 'I used the last of my savings before the wedding. I have not had reason to ask for a thing from St Aldric since.' She thought for a moment. 'Unless you are willing to take ladies' clothing, a pair of lovebirds or, perhaps, a horse. Go to the stables and tell them that I have given you Buttercup.'

'I do not need a horse,' he said firmly.

'It is just as well, for I do not wish to give her up. If it is money that you are after, then you will have to talk to the duke.'

'I have already spoken to him,' Richard said with confidence. 'And he leaves the decision to you.'

Damn the man. If she asked, St Aldric would give any sum she named to this interloper and he would be gone. But she suspected that whatever they had shared in the past months had been ruined by the fact that Richard had come here at all. She looked at him for a moment, wondering just what it was that she had seen in him, to hang so many dreams upon. And then she said, 'You wish my decision, Richard? Then here it is. If St Aldric thought you deserved money, you would have it already.'

'You mean to side with him, despite what he did to you in Dover?' Richard asked.

'I fail to see how my giving you a settlement would change the past,' she said as reasonably as possible. 'And since you made it clear just now that you would trade my love for gold, I am not inclined to give you either.'

'If I spoke in error,' he said, trying to look earnest, 'it was because I thought there was no other choice. You are more valuable to me than St Aldric's gold. It is only because I doubt you will leave him that I make the suggestion. St Aldric does not love you. If he did, he would not permit my presence in the house.'

Though she feared that half the words from Richard's mouth were lies, occasionally he found the truth.

'Not all marriages can be based on love,' she said, knowing that it was true. 'But we get on well enough together. That is more than many couples have.'

Richard was unimpressed. 'From what I hear from the people of this area, it should not be too difficult to get on well enough with St Aldric. I suspect it is his saintly nature that keeps him from reminding you of how oddly matched you are.'

'Perhaps so,' she retorted, 'but I notice that manners do not prevent you from mentioning it.'

Richard gave her a tired shake of his head. 'I merely wish you to remember what was obvious from the start. You are a governess, Maddie. And he is a duke. If not for the child you carry, he would not have looked twice at you. He would have chosen someone much more like Mrs Hastings. Someone from his social set.'

Perhaps it was true. But even though it would have been more appropriate, he had not married Evelyn.

Because she had turned him down.

Very well. Her husband did not love her. And perhaps they did not suit. She might have a future that held every material possession she might want. But it seemed strangely empty when she thought of the man who would share it—always polite, always solicitous, yet never truly hers. Maybe she would have to leave him. But not until she had placed the baby safe in his arms. Without thinking, she touched her belly again. *I do not want to leave you, as well,* she promised silently. *But we cannot always have what we want.*

Richard saw it and nodded. 'You are right to be thinking of the child. But it will be here soon, Maddie. And then what will you do?'

She did not know, so she could not answer.

Richard was looking at her as he had years ago, in the way that had made her believe in him. 'I know you do not want me here. And I know there will be no money. But I mean to stay until the baby is born. When it is come, if you wish it, I will see you safely away from here. I owe you that, at least, my dear. When you find that you can no longer bear to stay here, you need have nothing to fear. I will take care of you.' Then he pushed his plate aside, got up from his chair and came to her, kissing her once on the forehead before leaving her alone.

Chapter Seventeen

After the previous evening's activities, Michael did not expect to meet Richard Colver over breakfast. But it seemed that sleeping late after too much drink was not amongst the man's vices. When asked, Brooks relayed the information that Colver was already in the breakfast room with her Grace. Michael debated interrupting the pair of them and forcing his company upon them.

But then he remembered his fight with Madeline on the previous evening. If he had treated his wife with the kindness she deserved, there would be nothing to interrupt. She had told him she loved him. She had done it before, of course. But he had not wanted to hear it then. It was only when he thought he might not hear it again that he realised the value of those three little words.

She loved him. And he had refused to reciprocate.

Even now, he was still not sure that he could go to her and say the things she wanted to hear. He had made so many wild accusations that an apology was in order. But to follow it with the announcement that, he thought, perhaps, that he loved her? Even if he could deliver it with confidence, he doubted she would believe him. She would look at him as she sometimes did when she suspected that his thoughts did not match his words.

If nothing else, he did not wish to see Madeline in the company of Colver. Nor was he sure she'd want him under any circumstances. He would wait until after breakfast, and then he would find her and choose his words as carefully as an argument in the House of Lords. In the meantime, he would seek out his brother and get some of the familial advice that Eve thought was important. Sam knew more of love than he ever would. Surely he might be of some use on the subject.

When the servant showed him into the dower house, Sam was alone in the parlour. It was unusual, for he rarely saw the husband without the wife. Sam had explained that, after spending years separated from his true love, each moment with her was precious.

He had thought the devotion an admirable thing. But today it reminded him of his own wife and her supposed soulmate secluded in the breakfast room.

'Where is your wife this morning?' Michael said, trying not to scowl. 'After your excesses of last night, she has not run back to London without you, I trust?'

'Of course not.' Sam gave him the same knowing

smile he always wore, confident that, after years of waiting, Eve would have him drunk or sober. 'She is helping with a delivery in the village. But it is not too much longer that she will be helping at the main house. That is not why you are here, is it?'

To this, Michael could manage nothing more than a grunt.

'That is not the response I was expecting,' Sam said. 'You are the father-to-be. You have been badgering me with questions on the dreary details of human gestation for six months. But now that the race is almost run, you have lost interest?'

'I am not without interest,' Michael said. 'There are other things on my mind.'

'More important than the birth of your first child? Which, by my calculations, could occur at any moment?'

As a physician, Sam was not prone to exaggeration, but Michael suspected that, in this case, he might be guilty of it. Madeline had seemed fine on the previous evening, other than the fact that she had been furious with him.

'I am just as interested in the baby as I ever was,' he said. 'But at the moment, it is this Colver fellow that bothers me.'

'Then send him away,' Sam said with an incredulous shake of his head. 'You needn't be burdened with an uninvited guest at a time like this.'

'Madeline's guest,' Michael said.

'In your house,' Sam reminded him.

'But suppose she would rather that he stayed?'

Sam laughed. 'Has she told you this?'

'No,' Michael admitted.

Sam nodded. 'Then I assume you waited until Colver was dead drunk and we were gone, and had a terrific row about him. You said something supremely stupid to her, rather than sending him away when you had the chance. Now she is likely to cling to him out of spite to teach you the lesson you deserve.'

'Well, what am I to do about it?' Michael snapped. He did not like being read so easily.

'Apologise. Swear your love for her. Tell her that she must give up Colver or you will remove him yourself. And you can give her jewellery, I suppose. But I have never found that to be necessary when arguing with Evie.'

'Suppose I do not?' Michael asked.

'Do not what? Apologise? Then there is no hope for you. Whatever it was, it was likely your fault and you had best own up to it.'

'Suppose I do not love her?'

He could see by the shocked look on Sam's face that the possibility had not occurred to him. 'Then send the man away all the quicker. You do not want him in your house, and her feelings towards you, or him, do not matter.'

But even if he was not in love, he was sure her feelings did matter to him. 'When we married, I promised that she was to have her own way in all things.'

'I was there,' Sam reminded him. 'I thought it very foolish of you.'

'At the time, I was only concerned with getting her to agree to stay with me for the baby's sake. But now if she wants to go with Colver...'

'You wish to change your earlier agreement,' Sam said.

'I have grown used to her,' he admitted cautiously.

Sam snorted. 'You speak as though she were a hound or a pair of well-fitting boots.'

'It is more than that,' Michael said, trying to find the right words. 'She is pleasant company.'

'In what way?' Sam pressured. 'Do you think she makes an adequate partner at whist? Or do you simply enjoy lying with her?' Sam laughed again. 'Do not look so shocked at me. You are married to her after all. If you are intimate, it is as it should be.'

Michael was surprised. 'Is it so obvious?'

'To look at the pair of you, it is quite plain that yours has not been a marriage of convenience for some time,' Sam said. 'You dote on each other.'

'We do?' He tried to think of anything he might have done that would have lead to Sam's conclusion. 'While she is affectionate to me, it is nothing out of the bounds of propriety. I treat her with the courtesy that my wife deserves.'

'And when you are together, your eyes follow each other around the room. When you think we are not watching, you find any excuse to touch hands or stand too close to each other. If I linger too long over port after dinner, you begin yawning and making comments about the need for the duchess to get her rest.'

'She tires easily,' he insisted.

'She would need less sleep if you did not keep her up all night.'

Given a choice, he'd rather she take to afternoon naps than forgo their time together. 'You said that it was quite normal for breeding women to be affectionate,' Michael reminded him.

'Then you must be breeding, as well,' Sam concluded. 'I have not known you for long. But until recently, I have never seen you making calf's eyes at a woman, or staring at the door each time she leaves the room for a moment as though you cannot wait for her return.'

'I look at her no differently than I ever have,' Michael insisted.

'Not two days ago, I caught you feeding morsels to her from your plate and encouraging her to lick your fingers after each bite.'

'I worry when she does not eat,' he said, aware of how foolish it must sound.

'But that does not make it necessary to feed her by hand.' Sam shook his head. 'I would have stopped you had it not been so terribly amusing.'

'I doubt you will have source for such amusement in the future,' he said, remembering how they had parted. 'After the way I behaved last night, it would be safer to hand feed a tiger.'

'And if there was a tiger in the garden and she required you to feed it by hand, would you do it?'

Michael thought for a moment. 'If it made her smile, of course I would.'

'Then you have your answer as to your feelings for her,' Sam said with a nod. 'Now, take the advice of your personal physician. Go back to your wife and tell her of them. Nothing will cure your particular ailment of the heart but honesty in this one thing.' And with that, Sam dismissed him.

Michael walked back towards the house, still confused. While the doctor's simple instructions seemed like the right course of action, he could not help but think that there must be more to it. He had apologised to her before and could manage that without difficulty. If he remembered what Sam had said about his recent behaviour, he could announce his love for her with confidence.

But what if he told her to give up Colver and she refused? To put the man out of the house was to break his word—but to let him stay?

This was why he'd avoided love in the past. It led one to contemplate things that were intensely painful, like hand feeding tigers and entertaining one's wife's lover. Perhaps he had best go to the office and think about it for a while to find the right words. Or open the lock room and bring jewellery.

Or do neither. Madeline was waiting at the top of the stairs. Not for him, although it almost seemed that way. She was leaning against the wall, bending forward with her hands on her knees, as though she'd lost the strength to go farther.

He reached out to help her. 'Are you all right? Is it the baby?'

She looked at him strangely and shook off his offer of aid. 'Not all my problems are caused by the baby, you know.'

'Of course not.' Did she mean that he was a problem? Or was the problem that he seemed to care more about the child than the mother? 'I am sorry,' he said.

She closed her eyes and pulled herself up from the wall. 'I am just being difficult. I was winded after climbing the stairs. As you guessed, it was because of the baby. And I stopped to rest.'

'I am sorry for last night, as well,' he said. 'I said many things. And all of them were wrong.'

Now that the apology had passed, she was neither angry nor satisfied. She did not seem particularly interested in it either way.

'And I love you,' he added. Then he waited for the change that would make everything all right again.

She looked sorry for him, as though he'd tried his hardest and still could not learn the lesson she was teaching, but she said nothing in response. If this was how she'd felt when he had remained silent, he was beginning to understand the problem.

'About Colver,' he went on, meaning to get it all out at once before he lost his temper or his nerve.

'He means to stay until after the baby is born,' she

said, as though something had been settled without his knowledge. 'And I think that is probably for the best.'

What did she mean by that? If he was not the father, what use would Colver be? But to ask those questions would mean another argument. 'Sam said it could be very soon,' he said instead.

She nodded.

'He says you need your rest.' That had not been what he'd said at all. But it was probably true.

'I was going to lie down,' she agreed. 'I am not feeling well.'

Now that she mentioned it, she did not look well. But he did not mean to frighten her with it. 'It will all be over soon,' he said, hoping that it would comfort her.

Apparently it did not, for she was giving him the searching look she sometimes got when she was unsure of his meaning. Then she spoke. 'Before I go to my room, I have a question for you. If you could live life over again…'

It was the beginning of one of those rhetorical questions that women asked, which never seemed to end well. He braced himself for the worst.

'…would you have been happier marrying Evelyn?'

'Good God, no.' He had answered too quickly and too honestly. He corrected himself. 'She did not want me. She is in love with Sam.'

'But in all other ways, she would have been a better match,' Madeline informed him.

'Certainly not.'

'She would have been less trouble,' Madeline insisted. 'She knew your friends and they her. She would not have troubled you with lovebirds, or sad horses, or former lovers.'

'I love her dearly,' Michael said, embarrassed that the words came so easily when talking about someone other than his wife. 'But only as a sister. She'd have cheated on me with my own brother before the year was out. Not to mention that her manners are abominable and she refuses to change. In our one and only dinner together, she reduced one of the guests to apoplexy. And when I kissed her, I felt nothing.'

Madeline was smiling now. It was weak, but it was there. 'Apoplexy?'

He nodded. 'You have, on occasion, attempted to try my patience, but you are not nearly as successful as Evelyn can be. And she does it without even trying.'

The smile was gone and Madeline was looking strange again.

Perhaps he had misspoken again by criticising her friend. 'Would you like me to help you to your room?' he asked, for she was leaning against the wall again.

She shook her head again and turned down the hall of her wing with a vague wave of her hand, as though she could not be bothered with his help.

Apparently he was not needed. He did not like the feeling of being unnecessary in his own wife's life.

'Perhaps I shall see you at dinner,' he called after her. He would invite Sam and Evelyn as well, in case they were needed. Then he would go to the lock room and find some jewellery.

Chapter Eighteen

The bed in the duchess wing, for all its pillows and satin, was not conducive to restful sleep, but neither did Maddie want to open her eyes. She had dozed through the afternoon, but felt no better than she had when she'd lain down. The duke had sent up a pile of letters from prospective maids and nurses and nannies that she should be reading to prepare for the coming interviews. Apparently, when one was giving birth to the future Duke of St Aldric, a girl from the village would not do for even the simplest task.

Or perhaps it was just that St Aldric was still in a pet over Richard and trying to vex her with this. He had been most strange when she'd passed him in the hall earlier, apologising as he should have and talking no more nonsense about being tricked into marriage.

Then he'd announced, out of the blue, that he loved her, as if the only thing he'd got from the previous night's argument was that she expected to hear those particular words. But he had been wearing the same shallow smile that he used in the office and the drawing room, as though the event called for diplomacy and not passion.

The true Michael who hid behind her husband had not appeared until she'd asked him about Evelyn. For a moment or two, he had forgotten to be polite and seemed truly relieved that the engagement had failed. Then the courteous smile had returned and she had gone to her room.

And Richard, who she had longed to see for so long, would not go away. Did he not notice that she was near to bursting with another man's child? She'd have shouted the news to him before this, if the sweet little thing in her belly would allow her to take a breath. But his speech in the breakfast room that morning had been almost sincere once they had stopped talking about money. Perhaps he truly wanted nothing more than to help.

She had proven to her satisfaction that he had been wrong about Evelyn, of course. But there were so many things of which she was still unsure. Could she stand to live the whole of her life with a man who could not manage to feel for her?

Until she saw the baby, and its gender, and whether its birth would bring any real emotion to its father, she was not sure what she meant to do. By law, the child was his and her feelings for it did not matter. If she left, she must leave alone. That would mean leaving half her heart with the duke and the rest with her child. She would stay to be close to her son, even if it meant sacrificing her pride.

But suppose she had a daughter? There was no question that he would want a boy. But a girl might be little more than a disappointment to him, just as its mother seemed to be. She thought of her own childhood and the ever-present knowledge that, whatever it was her parents had wanted, she was not that thing.

No daughter of hers would feel unwanted, even for a moment. Perhaps St Aldric would let the two of them retire together from his life. The girl could be raised properly, with all the advantages of her birth and one parent who cherished her above all.

In either case, Maddie had no intention of welcoming the duke back to her bed without some indication of sincere feeling on his part. She would blame her past willingness on the vagaries of pregnancy and turn him out of the bedchamber. He had promised he would make no demands upon her. For the sake of her own breaking heart, she would hold him to his word.

It would not be too much longer before she had the answer. No matter the sex, the baby would come soon. Everyone kept telling her so. They had best be right, for Maddie could not stand much more of the physical misery that accompanied the emotional upheaval. If men did this to one, then they were more trouble than they were worth. She had long suspected it and now she was sure.

There was no comfort to be had in rising or sleeping. She was bloated and ugly. Today she did not feel well at all. And now there was a bumping in the walls, as if the largest rat in Aldricshire had located her bedroom with the intention of breaking up her peace. She had not noticed a similar problem in the nursery wing, thank goodness, but she would not risk bringing a child into a house full of vermin. If she could manage to get out of bed, she would go there with a broom and search. It would give her great pleasure to dispense any interlopers she found. Then she would take the broom to St Aldric for his foolishness in not allowing a terrier, or at least a cat, in the house to do the job for her. With all the little wire-and-wool animals in the nursery, there had been not a single one to be useful at a moment like this.

There was another thump and a rustle, and one of the hangings on the far wall rippled with the movement behind it. Maddie dragged herself to her feet, grabbed the only thing that came to hand, a bedroom slipper, and raised it over her head, advancing to strike.

Then the curtain pulled aside and a rather dusty Richard appeared, arms outstretched. 'My darling!'

'My God.' She yanked the fabric away to stare at the wood panel that had slipped to the side, revealing a narrow passageway behind the wall.

'I discovered the door pull in the wall of my chambers. Then I understood why you had been so insistent that I take that particular room.' He was smiling as if he'd found treasure and not just cobwebs. 'I knew if I but followed the passage that it would bring me to you.'

As if she'd have bothered with secret passages when she could have installed him next door for convenience. The thought of a more convenient Richard was almost as appalling as this sudden arrival in her room. It had been hard enough to breathe before, but the sudden shock of his appearance had taken the wind right out of her. 'What are you doing here?'

He looked at her as though it was the most obvious thing in the world. 'I have come to love you, my sweet.'

'I do not recall asking you to,' she said as reasonably as she could manage, pressing her hands to her stomach to settle the cramp. 'In fact, I have asked you to leave.'

'We agreed this morning that I was to stay until the baby was born,' he reminded her. 'I feared your feelings for me had cooled and you wanted nothing more than my friendship. But now that I discovered this?' He waved at the passageway behind him. 'It has all come clear to me.'

'Then you had best enlighten me,' she said, 'for I do not understand at all.'

'You wished for me to seek you out. To prove myself worthy of you.'

'You had years to find me,' she reminded him. 'I made it as easy as I could for you. Now you think that by crawling through a hole in my bedroom wall everything has changed?'

'But the time was not yet right to come for you,' he said with a smile. 'I had nothing to offer you.'

'Because you abandoned your commission and ran?' she said.

'I did not run.'

'Perhaps you walked, or rode,' she said, tired of the whole business. 'But if the Horse Guard thought you dead and you did not inform them otherwise, then I must assume you are a deserter.' She had thought his arrival in Aldricshire was an unpleasant shock. But it was nothing compared to this.

'You do not know what it was like,' he argued. 'Alone and friendless, so far from home.'

She laughed. 'Of all the arguments you might bring, my lack of sympathy for the lonely will do you the least good.'

For a moment, he did not look so sure of himself. Then the smile returned. 'But I have found my way back to you now.'

'You should have at least knocked,' she said. 'Or called out to explain yourself before entering my room.'

'At one time, you would not have minded,' he said. His sea-green eyes were as deep and beautiful as she remembered, but not as innocent.

'That was a long time ago,' she said. 'And I am married now.'

'But that is the wonder of it,' he said. 'Your husband has promised me that the decision is yours and he will deny you nothing. We can be together, even now.'

'If I wish it,' she reminded him.

'You do not have to tell him if you think it likely to upset him.' He pointed to the passageway again. 'We can love in secret, just as we used to.'

When they were young, he had assured her that secrecy was necessary to protect her honour. But now it was probably due to a very sensible fear of St Aldric. The duke's patience might wear thin once he discovered that there was a passage between the rooms.

She had a good mind to tell him of it.

'Love me now,' Richard insisted. 'Once the baby is born, you can be free of him. The child is all he wants from you. He told me so himself.'

Would St Aldric really say such a thing? Then the sudden pain she felt was her heart breaking.

Then she remembered that Richard was a terrible liar and she did not need to listen to him. The pain eased.

But Richard remained. 'Leave the baby with him,' he said. 'And come away with me as I suggested this morning. It will be as it was when we were first together.'

The idea that she would trade one moment with her own flesh and blood for a lifetime with Richard Colver took the last of her patience from her. Her body had no more space to contain the growing ire than it did to take a decent breath. 'This morning you spoke as my friend. Now you wish to be lovers. Before that, you wanted only my financial support because you claimed I had ruined your prospects.'

'And I will still need your help,' he admitted. 'But if you separate from your husband, he will not make you live without funds.'

'You wish me to leave him because when I do, he will support me and I will support the pair of us?'

'You make it sound so sordid, my dove.' He reached for her again.

'Because it is,' she said, tapping him lightly on the forehead with the slipper she had been holding. 'Have you no desire to supply for your own needs?'

He sighed. 'The life of a veteran is not a happy one. Many of us are begging in the street.'

'Those who are missing an arm or a leg, perhaps. Those who are unfit to work.' Had Richard ever spoken of a job? He'd had a nebulous plan to make his fortune while in the army. He had talked often enough of his father's unfairness. But even now she was sure that Mr Colver would take him back, should he decide to return to the family business.

He gave her a pitiable look. 'I will, of course, apply myself to some job or other. It is simply a matter of finding one that is suitable. Until that time, my sweet pigeon, I see no reason why we cannot begin our life together.'

'Oh, Richard,' she said, shaking her head, with a smile. 'There is one very good reason.'

'What is that, my little chicken?'

'Because while I might wish to leave my husband,

I do not wish to leave my baby. And I would not trade either of them for another moment with you. Now pack your things and go to…Norfolk. Or to Hades. Really, I do not care.' She did not feel up to having this discussion. In fact, she rather thought that it would be nice to crawl back into bed and die.

'But my dear duckling, my…'

And that was the last straw. Ducks waddled. Now so did she. She turned and grabbed the first handy thing, a bolster trimmed with gold tassels, and swung it at him. 'I am not your little duckling. I am not a bird of any kind and especially not a lovebird. Most important, I am not yours.'

Richard dodged the pillow and stepped farther into the room, towards the bed. 'You are speaking of the marriage to the duke? Do not be silly…angel.'

It was not a bird, but it still had wings. She grabbed a hairbrush from the vanity and threw it at his head.

'You were mine long before you were his.' He was circling the room, trying to get close to her again. 'And glad to be so, as I remember it.'

'Because I loved you,' she said. The words seemed to cramp inside her, as though the baby and everything else about her rebelled at the knowledge.

Richard, merely looked surprised. 'When I left you, you had no trouble forgetting me. You have tumbled into quite the downy nest, while I have not a feather to fly with.'

More feathers. She gave an inarticulate growl of disgust and looked for something else to throw.

He held out his arms to block her aim and took another step forward. 'You cannot mean to send me away so soon. To forget the love we shared. To separate yourself from your oldest and dearest friend?'

'We are no longer friends,' she said. Today she did not feel friendly to anyone, and even less so to Richard. 'Nor are we lovers.'

'But we can be again, can we not? We could start fresh.' He put down his hands and smiled at her as he used to, when she was young and trusting. Then he added, 'It would be quite safe to be so, for you are already with child.'

'St Aldric…'

'Is on the other side of the house and will not hear a thing,' he said, his smile changing to an evil grin. 'And you are more than enough woman to handle the two of us.'

If that comment was meant to reflect on her current size, there would be hell to pay. She grabbed another pillow and swung with all her might for his head. When it struck, the seam split in a burst of feathers, but the exertion left her short of breath and clasping her middle.

'Not that you are unattractive,' he said, sensing his misstep. 'You are the very bloom of health. Lovelier than you have ever been. Now, what say you to a tumble?' He made another lunge for her, sprawling on the bed.

She grabbed the first thing handy, the heavy brass

candlestick on the bedside table and swung it like a club, catching him in the shoulder.

'Out.'

'My... Ow.' Her next blow had taken him before he could find another avian endearment.

'Out,' she said, brandishing the candlestick. 'Now. From this room, from this house. Do not wait for your things. They will be sent after.'

'But I am willing to wait,' he said, hands on his heart. 'A lifetime, if necessary.'

She took another swing. Except for the pain in her stomach, it felt good. 'And that might not be so very long,' she said, waving her makeshift club in front of her. 'If you do not go now, you will end this day covered from head to toe in bruises. And do not think you will not.' She swung again, catching him another thump to the arm, which actually raised a look of alarm.

'I will not leave you,' he insisted, dodging the next blow. 'Call the servants if you must. It will be quite embarrassing when they find us in the middle of a lovers' spat.' But he did not look quite as sure as he had.

She shook her head and smiled as a mad idea occurred to her. 'Waiting for the servants would take too long. I am breeding, as you say. And my moods are...volatile.' She swung again and he actually rolled away onto the floor, scrambling to put the bed between them.

'Now, now, Maddie....'

She threw the candlestick and watched it bounce

off his shoulder before searching about for something else to pitch at him. 'You want my company, do you, Richard? After all this time? You returned from the war and did not rush to me while I was still young and sweet-tempered. Well, you have found me now—and how do you like me?' She sent a paperweight from the desk sailing past his head and into the cheval glass behind him. It hit with a resounding crack and half the mirror slid from the frame to shatter on the rug.

'For God's sake, Maddie! Have you lost your mind?' He turned to back towards the salon door, finding it locked and muttering, 'Damn.'

'Perhaps I had no mind to begin with,' she said, on fire with pain and evil glee. 'But I know you are right in one thing. I am more than enough woman for the pair of you.' The porcelain ornament she grabbed next caught him in the forehead, raising a trickle of blood before it bounced away.

'Ask the duke—he will tell you how much trouble I am. A tartar, a shrew, a fishwife. I have taken each opportunity I could find to make his life a misery. Your arrival here is just one example.' She grabbed the poker from the fireplace and hefted it in her hand. 'And the thing is, Richard, I am quite fond of him. One might even say that I love him. He did not dishonour and abandon me as you did.'

She brandished the poker like a sword. 'Oh, my first beloved—' she swung '—my duckling—' she swung again '—my fine proud cockerel.' She smiled, advancing on him. 'People keep telling me that I have an increased appetite. But I think it might be for violence. If you do not have the sense to leave me this instant, you will be a capon when I am finished with you. And the duke and all his servants will not lift a finger to help you.'

With that, her one true beloved turned and ran down the passage to his room and slammed the door behind him.

Chapter Nineteen

Maddie summoned Peg, who looked in horror at the destruction in the room. 'Throw it all away,' she said, waving her arms wide. 'And tear down the draperies, as well. Then tell a footman to nail the walls shut.'

'Beggin' your pardon, your Grace?' The maid looked at her as though she had made the sort of mad comment that one would expect from a tosser of pillows or a breaker of glass.

'And see to it that Mr Colver is removed from the house. Immediately.'

'Very good, your Grace.' This, at least, made some sense.

With the removal of Richard settled, Maddie staggered towards her husband's office before the next pain could come again.

'St Aldric! I demand to speak to you this instant!'

Seeing her expression, Upton immediately began gathering his notebooks to retreat. But the smile that the duke gave her was as neutral and unperturbed as ever, as though he did not wish to air their troubles in front of the staff. 'Yes, my love?'

'Do not mock me with endearments,' she said, grabbing the corner of the desk. She caught her breath and spoke again. 'This house is…unsatisfactory.'

'Really?' Now he was drawling. She had never known him to drawl, even on the days when he had been most impatient with her. 'Whatever is the problem, my dear? Would you like something larger? If I could convince the Regent to let us Carlton House—but it might not be big enough to hold your wardrobe.' He was teasing her and she was in no mood for it.

'This one will do nicely, once it has been gutted and redone,' she said, glaring at him. 'Do not give me that look as though you do not know the problems here, for it is plain that you do not like it either.'

'I will admit to no such thing,' he said, glancing at Upton as though to remind her of the need for manners. 'It is my boyhood home, you know.'

'And I do not wish to stay another night in it.'

'We will return to London in a week, or perhaps less,' he said as reasonably as possible. 'But I doubt Evelyn will encourage you to travel at this time. And you must remember that you have a guest.' He rolled his eyes upwards. Then he went white as a thought occurred to him. 'Or does he mean to take you away…?'

So the idea that she might leave with Richard had struck him dumb. She wished that she felt well enough to enjoy the fact, but now he was grabbing at her arm.

She was sure that if she tried to leave, he would re-strain her.

Then another pain took her and she stood gasping for a moment, forcing out words in short, breathless sentences:

'I sent Richard away.'

'He came into my room.'

'Through a passage in the wall.'

Her discomfort went unnoticed, but the words caught his attention. While his expression did not really change, she saw the impassive mask drop away as he stared into her face. 'He what?' She could feel the muscles beneath his coat sleeve tensing as though he was preparing for a fight.

She caught her breath again. 'He entered my room without my permission. I do not even allow you to do so.'

The duke had always been a tall man, but he seemed to grow even taller with outrage at the of-fence to her. His arm was as taut as a bowstring, ready to let fly. 'And where is Colver now?' There was murder in his blue eyes and his smile was thin, angry and very, very real.

She would remember to be thrilled by the response, but later, when she was not so preoccupied. She could feel the next pain, waiting, only moments away. 'I do not know. The servants have probably removed him by now. But I dealt with him myself. Some things in my room were broken.'

'Things?'

'A paperweight, a mirror, some assorted crockery. I was upset,' she said, gasping as though she was about to be pulled underwater. 'It took some time to perfect my aim.'

His lips twitched. Then he said, very softly, 'I think I was very fortunate that the rooms in Dover were devoid of ornament. I deserved a thrashing that night.'

The pain took her again and her next words came out in a squeak. 'You deserve one now, for you are responsible for the miserable state I am in.'

'The state you are in?'

'You dolt.' This time, the pain was strong enough that she lost her breath and could barely mouth the words. 'If you ask Evelyn…she will tell you more than you want to know…. It has been nearly nine months and two weeks since Dover.'

'They said soon,' he agreed.

It was a shame that a man who was so beautiful could be so dense. The pressure had eased a little and she took a breath and spoke again. 'Two weeks too long. I have been ready for at least a month. But the baby waited until now.'

'Now?'

She clutched the desk as the pain subsided and her knees went weak. 'Now. But that does not mean that I will forget the inadequacies of this abomination of a house.'

'Now.' He seemed fixated on the one word. 'We must get you to your room immediately.'

'You are not listening to me,' she said, slapping

him on the biceps. 'I do not want to go to my room.'
She dug the nails of her other hand into the wood of
his desk, both for support and because she was afraid
he would send her away before she could finish what
she was saying. 'I hate my room. I will not go back
there. It is full of broken glass.'

'One of the guest rooms, then.' He reached for her
arm again, trying to guide her away from the matter at hand.

'The whole wing is ridiculous. Rooms upon rooms.
All leading to each other. Secret passages and lovers
like mice in the walls.' The pain took her again and
she started to double.

She got a brief look at Upton, who was still in the
room with them, caught between amazement and terror.

She balled her fists and pounded them against the
rigid muscles of her stomach, begging them to loosen.

But the duke's hand caught hers, pulling her back
into his chest, wrapping himself around her in a protective shell. 'Of course, darling. I am sorry that I
brought you here. Upton,' he said, in the proper duke's
voice that did not sound at all like the real Michael
who was holding her. 'Prepare a budget, find an architect and hire some carpenters. We will wish to begin
in a week, perhaps two.'

'Immediately,' she insisted. 'It must be totally redone. We must have a main corridor as decent houses
do. And normal bedchambers beside each other. Yours
is extremely inconvenient.'

He was walking her slowly towards the door. 'Perhaps it is your room that is the inconvenient one. But now that you have ruined it by tossing crockery about, we will find you another place. Near to me.'

'Your wing is no better. You sleep in a brothel.' She caught her breath and freed her hands, making an expansive gesture towards the second floor. 'Atrocious decorating and the smell of tobacco smoke and liquor. And opium.'

'I agree,' he said, moving a little more quickly. In an aside to the overseer, he whispered, 'Get Dr Hastings and his wife. Quickly, man.' He turned back to her. 'I am sure the housekeeper would take exception to the statements about cleanliness. The rooms have been aired.'

'I am extremely sensitive,' she reminded him. 'And I know what went on there. It cannot be cleaned. It reeks of sin.' She pointed a dire finger in the direction of the back of the house. 'Only the nursery is bearable.'

'Then that is where I shall take you,' he said, kissing her hair.

'Not until you have removed the lock.'

'I will have the lock struck off at once, as soon as you are settled,' he agreed. 'But now we must get you to bed.'

She felt her abdomen begin to tighten and clung more tightly to his neck. 'There is no point in a door there at all. We will not cage this child like an animal, Michael.'

'Michael,' he murmured, as though he had never

heard his own name before. His hands were messaging her back, pressing deeply against knots of muscles that did not want to release.

'What if there was a fire? And we could not get to the baby….' She gave a small sob, for the thought frightened her and she hurt. 'And he was trapped there…with that silly little farm.'

'We will put it away,' he agreed.

She could not seem to stop the tears and the pain was still coming, even longer and harder than the last one. 'Blast and damn.'

He started at her exclamation.

'I have had care of boys, Michael. It is not as if I have never heard the words before.'

'I see.' He was smiling at her.

'And this hurts,' she reminded him.

'Of course, my love.' He stooped to get a hand behind her knees and scooped. Suddenly she was in his arms, being carried quickly towards the second floor.

'I can walk,' she said, kicking her feet.

'You have had care of boys, Madeline, but you have never had a baby. Let me help you.'

'Very well.' But she feared, before this was over, that the majority of the process would fall totally to her.

'Evelyn will be here soon and she will take care of the rest.'

'And we should have real pets for the children, not wood and wire. You may not think so, but they are both sanitary and good company for a child. You must procure a pup from the stables. And let one of the kittens from the kitchen be brought up to the bedroom to keep the rats out of the cradle.'

'I will get them at once, my dear. As soon as we have got you to bed.'

That would probably be for the best. The pain and the hurry were making things very confusing. Michael wasn't himself at all. Or perhaps he was very much himself. She was forgetting which was which. But at least he had listened to her complaints. When he put her down, it was in the governess's room in the now-doorless nursery wing. The sheets were clean and the coverlet was soft cotton, without the nonsense of satin and ribbons that would be hard to clean.

He sat her down on the edge of the mattress and helped her out of her clothing, then called for Peg to bring her a clean nightrail, slipping it over her head, and then sliding her into the bed.

He sat by her side, stroking her hand and wiping her brow until Evelyn came and chased him away so that they might get down to the serious business of having the next duke.

It seemed an eternity since Maddie had come into his office raving like a madwoman. But by Sam's watch it had been only twelve hours, which he claimed was neither too long nor too short.

Now they sat together on the top stair, waiting. Michael had waved away suggestions that they retire to the library and had refused the chairs that the servants offered to set for them in the corridor. It did not seem right that he should wait in comfort while she suffered for something he had caused to happen. But he wished that he had not succumbed to her demand to remove the nursery door. The extra layer of wood might have blocked some of his wife's cries.

It was small comfort that Colver was not here to get in the way. But damn them both. He would haul the blighter back, relinquish his bride and make the fellow marry her if it would ease her labour.

But she had called him Michael. And she had done it more than once. She had been in pain, and she had come to him for help, calling him by his given name.

The thought made him grin. He wanted to move heaven and earth for her. He would have to find a quiet place for mother and child to rest while the remodelling was done. Or he could simply demand that the workmen proceed in complete silence. Compared to housing a dozen tropical birds, how hard could it be to close up a few doors?

Maddie cried out again and the breath stopped in his throat as he waited for the shrinking silences between the pains. The uncomfortable, bony feeling of the mahogany beneath him was a small penance. And the baluster he gripped anchored him to the spot when he felt like fleeing for the brandy decanter.

'It will not be much longer,' Sam said. He was far too comfortable with the whole process, but the sounds of the cries were not ripping out his heart, because they did not come from his wife.

'How can you know how long it will take?'

'I have seen deliveries before.'

'Each one was the same, then?'

Sam paused. 'No. Each is unique. But you have nothing to fear with Evelyn there.'

'And this midwife wife of yours—' he released the newel post long enough to gesture towards the closed door '—has she been 100 per cent successful in her job?'

Sam paused. The silence was answer enough. The silence coming from the childbed was equally bad. The cries had been loud but regular. What did it mean that they had stopped?

'That's it. I am going to see her.'

'You must not.' Sam grabbed at his arm to pull him back down on the stair. 'There is no room for you there. Let Evelyn get on with her work. They will send for you when it is over.'

When it was over. What the devil did that mean? If he waited until it was over, there was a chance that he might have waited too long. He would lose her and she would never know how he felt. Sam hurried past him and stood in the doorway of the nursery, trying to prevent his entering. But blood did not give him the right to stand between a duke and what he wanted. Michael pushed past and through the door.

Maddie stared up at the crack in the ceiling and waited for the pain to stop. But the pain never seemed to stop now. It just rose and fell like waves, and the troughs were shallower and shallower. She was sure she had seen that crack in the plaster before, in happier times. But the laudanum made it hard to remember when.

'You cannot be here, your Grace. You will not wish to see.' Evelyn was using her firm and matronly voice. And she was trying to shoo a duke.

What a ludicrous idea. In Maddie's experience, dukes were very hard to shoo. Another contraction took her, and took her breath, locking her body in a vice, squeezing.

'Michael. Come away. This is no place for you.'

Sam was here, as well? Was everyone to witness this? Could she have no privacy at all? All she wished was to be alone. To crawl into the woods like an animal and wrap herself around this pain until it stopped.

'Bollocks. Get out of my way, the pair of you.' She heard the scrape of a chair, but could not manage to turn her head towards it. If she did, she was sure that the world would be on fire to match the pain she was feeling. Even now, the edges of her vision were red like blood, the crack in the plaster running like a river through a burning city. She shut her eyes to protect them from the flames.

'Madeline. Do not die!'

As if Michael could command even that. He was only a duke. She wanted to laugh, but she had not the breath for it.

But she knew he was with her, clutching her hand so hard that her fingers hurt. And for a moment, it was the only real point she could find, beyond the agony of the next contraction. She focused on it, letting it hold her to the earth.

'I am sorry. So very sorry for causing this. You need never go through it again.' A hand smoothed her forehead, wiping the hair back. 'Just the once. It will be over soon. I am here.'

How did he know? He was not a doctor. Nor was he a midwife. But what good had either of those been to her in the past few hours? She was alone, all alone with this.

Then she felt the squeeze of his hand again and she squeezed back. Or tried, at least. Another contraction took her and all the strength left her arm, directed elsewhere as though her entire body was a fist.

'Never again. You will be free if you wish. A life of luxury. Comfort. No pain, I swear. No more pain.'

How was that to be managed? she wondered. Death was the only end to pain. The idea was strangely appealing. Quiet. Dark. Silent. Painless.

'Madeline!' His voice dragged her back in time for another pain. Everything was red again, loud, sharp and hurtful. 'Do not leave me. Please. Not now. You may have your freedom tomorrow. But not until you are done with this.'

As though what she was doing was a small task. And he seemed so sure it would end. To her it felt like it would go on for ever.

'Maddie! Maddie! Stay with me. I love you.'

He could not have said it. It was a dream and the words were conjured from what she wanted to hear.

'I love you, Madeline. Damn it, woman. Do you hear me? I love you. And I will never stop telling you so. But you must come back to me so that you can hear me say it.'

'There!' Evelyn seemed pleased with something, God knew what, but the midwife had come to her other side and was leaning close, over her face.

'Maddie. Open your eyes. Just for a moment.'

She tried. Evelyn looked quite mad and nearly as dishevelled as she felt. When she turned her head, Michael looked even worse. The smile he gave her did not help at all.

'Push,' Evelyn said, low and urgent. 'When the next contraction comes, push with it. Let your body tell you what to do.'

Everything about her squeezed. But there was a pressing downward. She was making horrible animal noises.

It stopped. She gasped for breath. This was easier. She tried to speak, but there was no energy for it. She nodded to Michael, panting, unsure of what she was agreeing to. But a nod was all she could manage.

He smiled and nodded back, encouraging.

'Push.' Evelyn was nearly as commanding as a duke. And much easier to obey.

'Oh, my God.' Michael seemed shocked. But when she looked to him, he was smiling.

'It is perfectly normal, your Grace.' Evelyn, still

calm and in control. And then to her, 'We see the head, Maddie. A few more minutes. That is all we need from you. Then you can rest.'

Rest would be good. Another push came. Like the tide. She went with it. Evelyn was gone from her side, but Michael did not leave. He shot nervous glances to her belly and back to her face. Then he grinned. He looked very foolish and totally undignified.

'Again, your Grace. Again.'

'Do not call me that!' she managed to shout at Evelyn. There was nothing graceful about this. She pushed again.

There was a cry.

It was not hers.

And a shout of triumph from her husband as though he had done any of the work.

She fell back into the pillows. 'The baby?'

'Let me take her. Let me.'

Evelyn's laugh. 'Let me clean her first, Michael. Then she will go to her mother.'

Her?

But why was St Aldric so happy?

'We have a daughter,' Michael said, kissing her on the forehead. Once. Twice. Again. 'We have a daughter. And, save her mother, she is the most beautiful woman I have ever seen.'

There was a heavy weight in her arms. Warm. Soft. And it was moving.

She slept.

Chapter Twenty

When Maddie woke, her husband had not moved from her side. From somewhere, she heard a faint mewling and felt another squeeze of her hand. 'Michael?' She was hoarse from crying out. And if she looked the way she felt, hot and damp and worn out, then she must truly be a fright to behold. She should send the duke away and summon her maid to repair the damage. A mirror would surely tell her that she did not look like a duchess at all.

But he did not seem to mind. Without a word, he put an arm behind her back and held her, steadying a cup as she drank. He was cradling her close against him, just as she would hold an infant, and looking at her as though she were the most precious thing in the world.

'Where?' She leaned up, trying to see the baby. It felt strange. She was weak, but she felt weightless, as if she was floating in a pond.

'The nurse will bring her to you shortly. But you must rest.'

'Her?' He had said daughter. Then he'd called her beautiful.

He was smiling in a way she had not seen before, like a man utterly besotted. 'Could we, perhaps, name her Eleanor? It was my mother's name.'

And now, apparently, he was thinking fondly of his mother. God knew why, for they could not have been close. It was strange that he should ask, as though she was to be allowed an opinion. Strange that he should even care, after all the fuss he had made about an heir. 'You needed a son,' she reminded him. She looked eagerly towards the door. Right now, she wanted nothing more than to know that little Eleanor was healthy and safe. 'I will give you one next time. Now let me see my little girl.'

'You must not speak of a next time,' he said softly. 'This was too hard for you. I will not see you suffer again.'

'How else will we have a boy?' she said, still staring at the doorway to catch the first glimpse of her daughter.

'As I told you when I married you, I will find another way. But do not fear for Eleanor. She will be treated like a princess.'

'Of course she will,' Maddie agreed.

'And she shall have both a puppy and a kitten, just as you wished.'

She did not remember wishing for any such thing.

But her memory of the past day or so was cloudy. Except for one thing. 'You said you loved me?'

'I adore you,' he said, kissing her hair. 'You are my life. And that is why I will not risk you again. No more children, Maddie. I could not stand to go through this again.'

She waved the idea away. 'One child is not enough. Eleanor will want a playmate, or perhaps two or three.'

Michael looked doubtful and opened his mouth as if to refuse her again.

Maddie gave him a stern look. 'If it bothers you so, next time I will not let you watch. But I mean to do it again. Not today, of course. But in a year or two. It will be much less frightening now that we have done it once.'

'Shh.' He laid a hand against her shoulder, pushing her back onto the bed. 'Do not agitate yourself. You are still weak.'

She tried to sit up again. 'Not so weak that I will let you cast me off.'

'I am not casting you off,' he said patiently, then leaned in and kissed her forehead. 'I promised you your freedom from the very first. I will not hold you here and make you suffer just so that I might have an heir.'

There was no reasoning with the man. And so she grabbed his dishevelled cravat and dragged his face to hers for a kiss. For one who would forswear her company for her own good, he was not fighting very hard to resist her now. His mouth tasted salty, like sweat and tears, and he did not kiss at all like a proper duke. Instead, he responded with all the joy in his heart. She liked it very well. 'If you want no more children, we will not have the fun of making one,' she said when she was through with him.

'But you will be so busy with the renovations that you will hardly have time for me.'

'I will?' she said absently, touching his beautiful lips with her fingertip.

'You came into my office, raving about the need to tear down the walls and start afresh. It was after you turned out your precious Richard.'

'Richard was not the least bit precious,' she admitted. 'Richard was an ass. He took horrible advantage of me, then acted as though I owed him for the privilege. He was quite horrible and I wasted years of my life waiting for him.'

'And that is why I found you,' Michael said. 'So he was not totally without worth.'

'But I did not know what a devil he was until I married a saint.'

'I am not a saint,' he reminded her, still frustrated by the label.

'Of course not, Michael. You are as prone to mistakes as the rest of us. Because you are flesh and blood.' And what glorious flesh it was. Even the exhaustion of giving birth had not totally dulled her desire for the man leaning over her bed.

'And I was not raving when I came into your office,'

she added. 'I was merely expressing my opinions adamantly, because I was frustrated. And in pain.'

His expression softened immediately when she mentioned pain, and he rubbed his face against their clasped hands.

Who knew the man had such a weakness for her comfort? 'It was far more difficult for you to watch the pain than for me to experience it,' she said, and gave him a sympathetic look. 'And really, you shouldn't have been there. Men are too delicate for childbirth. It is why God has given the job to women.'

The idea shocked him to silence.

So she leaned forward and captured his lips, turning the contact into another delicious kiss. When she leaned back to look at his face, she was reminded yet again what a handsome man her husband was. And how lucky she was to have that Adonis wrapped around her little finger.

Then the nurse brought their daughter to them. And Michael had been right. She was the most beautiful girl that Maddie had ever seen, with deep blue eyes and a wisp of blonde hair. 'She looks like you,' Maddie whispered. 'And Eleanor is a lovely name. Now that I have her, my life is almost perfect.'

'Almost?' He pretended to sigh. 'How will I manage, now that I have two ladies to make unreasonable demands upon me?'

'You needn't worry about one of us, for your daughter will not even talk for a year or two.' Maddie smiled.

'But you did promise me that I could have whatever wanted if I married you.'

'I did,' he agreed. 'And what do you command o me now, your Grace?'

'I want your heart, for the rest of my life.'

'You have it, my love.'

She ran her hand up his chest and let that finge slide beneath his neckcloth until she found a bit o bare skin to touch. 'And your body, as well.'

He swallowed nervously, but he nodded.

'And I want you to give me a house full of children who all look like you.' Then she kissed him agair to make him forget what an enormous house it was.

* * * * *

REQUEST YOUR FREE BOOKS!

 HARLEQUIN® HISTORICAL:
Where love is timeless

2 FREE NOVELS PLUS 2 FREE GIFTS!

YES! Please send me 2 FREE Harlequin® Historical novels and my 2 FREE gifts (gifts are worth about $10). After receiving them, if I don't wish to receive any more books, I can return the shipping statement marked "cancel." If I don't cancel, I will receive 6 brand-new novels every month and be billed just $5.44 per book in the U.S. or $5.74 per book in Canada. That's a savings of at least 16% off the cover price! It's quite a bargain! Shipping and handling is just 50¢ per book in the U.S. and 75¢ per book in Canada.* I understand that accepting the 2 free books and gifts places me under no obligation to buy anything. I can always return a shipment and cancel at any time. Even if I never buy another book, the two free books and gifts are mine to keep forever.

246/349 HDN F4ZY

Name _____ (PLEASE PRINT) _____

Address _____ Apt. # _____

City _____ State/Prov. _____ Zip/Postal Code _____

Signature (if under 18, a parent or guardian must sign)

Mail to the **Harlequin® Reader Service:**
IN U.S.A.: P.O. Box 1867, Buffalo, NY 14240-1867
IN CANADA: P.O. Box 609, Fort Erie, Ontario L2A 5X3

Want to try two free books from another line?
Call 1-800-873-8635 or visit www.ReaderService.com.

* Terms and prices subject to change without notice. Prices do not include applicable taxes. Sales tax applicable in N.Y. Canadian residents will be charged applicable taxes. Offer not valid in Quebec. This offer is limited to one order per household. Not valid for current subscribers to Harlequin Historical books. All orders subject to credit approval. Credit or debit balances in a customer's account(s) may be offset by any other outstanding balance owed by or to the customer. Please allow 4 to 6 weeks for delivery. Offer available while quantities last.

Your Privacy—The Harlequin® Reader Service is committed to protecting your privacy. Our Privacy Policy is available online at www.ReaderService.com or upon request from the Harlequin Reader Service.

We make a portion of our mailing list available to reputable third parties that offer products we believe may interest you. If you prefer that we not exchange your name with third parties, or if you wish to clarify or modify your communication preferences, please visit us at www.ReaderService.com/consumerchoice or write to us at Harlequin Reader Service Preference Service, P.O. Box 9062, Buffalo, NY 14269. Include your complete name and address.

HHI3R

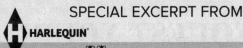
*Next month, get swept away by Rhys Denham and
Lady Thea as they embark on a journey of adventure,
passion and discovery...*

Rhys sighed and moved his mouth gently against the head
of the woman in his arms. This was the way to wake up.
Warm, rocking gently, arms full of soft, curvaceous femininity.

She smelled of roses, whoever she was. He must try to
recall her name in a minute; it was ungentlemanly to forget
in the morning. Not that he could recall the night before
either, but he supposed it must have been good. His body
was certainly awake and interested.

When he pulled her more tightly against him she snuggled back with an erotic little wriggle that inflamed him to
aching point.

"Mmm." Rhys nuzzled the silky-fine hair and let his right
hand stray lightly across her body. They were both dressed,
after a fashion, although their bare feet had obviously made
friends in the night. Perhaps she had pulled on her gown
again afterward for warmth, because under the fine wool
he could feel uncorseted curves and the sweet weight of an
unfettered breast. As his thumb moved across the nipple it
hardened, and he smiled.

His companion stirred, stretched, her feet sliding down
against his. She yawned and he came completely awake. He
was in the chaise, on the ship, heading for France, and in his
arms, pressed against him, her breast cupped in his hand,
was Lady Althea Curtiss.

Rhys bit back the word that sprang to his lips and went very still. Was she awake? Had she realized? Probably no or she'd be screaming the place down or, given that this wa Thea, applying that sharp elbow where it would do mos harm. He let his hand fall away from her breast, lifted th other from her hip and arched his midsection as far bac as he could. If he tried to slide his arm from under her sh would probably wake.

Damn it. *Thea,* the innocent, respectable friend whom h had already shocked with that embrace.

Rhys thought about Almack's, tripe and onions, Lati verbs, tailors' accounts. It didn't work. His brain, appar ently having lost all its blood in a mad southward dash was disobediently musing on just where Thea had acquire those curves from and when she had begun to smell of rose and how that mousy mane of hair could be so silky.

"Rhys?" His name was muffled in a yawn.

Don't miss
UNLACING LADY THEA by Louise Allen
available from Harlequin® Historical April 2014.

HARLEQUIN®

HISTORICAL

Where love is timeless

COMING IN APRIL 2014

Welcome to Wyoming
by Kate Bridges

Seeking justice for his murdered colleagues, Detective Simon Garr has gone undercover as infamous jewel thief Jarrod Ledbetter. All is going to plan, until he finds out that Jarrod's mail-order bride is on her way to Wyoming! Simon can't afford to jeopardize his cover, and he's left with only one option—he must marry the woman!

When his poor bride Natasha O'Sullivan arrives she doesn't have a clue what she is walking into—but Simon finds there is more to her than first meets the eye. Because Natasha has brought along secrets of her own....

Mail-Order Weddings
From blushing bride to Wild West wife!

Available wherever books and ebooks are sold.

HH29779

HISTORICAL

Where love is timeless

COMING IN APRIL 2014

London's Most Wanted Rake
by Bronwyn Scott

Rumor has it that Channing Deveril, founder of
The League of Discreet Gentlemen, is tired of warming women's
beds. But when he encounters the alluring Alina Marliss, the
stage is set for his most ambitious assignment yet....

Alina is accustomed to teetering on the edge of scandal, so
Channing's skillful seduction is a complication she definitely
doesn't need! She might crave his expert touch, but she has no
intention of losing her head—much less her heart—over
London's most notorious rake!

Rakes Who Make Husbands Jealous
Only London's best lovers need apply!

Available wherever books and ebooks are sold.

HISTORICAL

Where love is timeless

The Wedding Ring Quest
by Carla Kelly

Penniless Mary Rennie knows she's lucky to have a home in Edinburgh, but she does crave more excitement in her life. So when her cousin's ring is lost in one of several fruitcakes heading round the country as gifts, Mary seizes the chance for adventure.

When widowed captain Ross Rennie and his son meet Mary in a coaching inn, they take her under their wing. After years of battling Napoleon, Ross's soul is war-weary, but Mary's warmth and humor touch him deep inside. Soon, he's in the most heart-stopping situation of his life—considering a wedding-ring quest of his own!

Coming in April 2014

Available wherever books and ebooks are sold.

Love the Harlequin book you just read?

Your opinion matters.

Review this book on your favorite
book site, review site, blog or your own
social media properties and share
your opinion with other readers!